Guy N. Sm̶...........................books,
runs a mai...........................rare
SF, horror a...........................mall-
holding on th...........................ne he
sleeps. He is...........................dren.

By the same author

GUY N. SMITH

The Sucking Pit

GRAFTON BOOKS

A Division of the Collins Publishing Group

LONDON GLASGOW
TORONTO SYDNEY AUCKLAND

Grafton Books
A Division of the Collins Publishing Group
8 Grafton Street, London W1X 3LA

Published by Grafton Books 1989

First published in Great Britain by
New English Library 1975

ISBN 0-586-20495-4

Printed and bound in Great Britain by
Collins, Glasgow

Set in Century Schoolbook

To J. D. who knows the legend

1

The fox paused at the top of the steeply wooded rise. His body, mingling with the autumnal colourings, was heaving and his breath came quickly. Behind him he could hear the excited baying of the hounds. For a moment fear was plainly visible in his vulpine eyes, but this gave way to puzzlement. The hounds had *never* come in the wood before. He didn't know why, but they always stopped at the lower boundary in answer to the horn which summoned them back to their masters.

Not so today. They were in full cry. Reynard looked at the grassy basin which lay below him. Its sides were emerald green, sloping steeply down to an acre or so of level ground. It was soft and marshy. Usually he avoided it, having seen a hare which he was chasing disappear beneath its squelchy surface. Yet there *was* a way across. Those two clumps of spiky grass and the willow sapling, if followed in a completely straight line, led reasonably safely to the opposite slope. Reynard knew he would just about make it. Anything or anybody heavier . . .

He waited another minute or so. The baying

came closer every second. Then he saw the leading hound, a massive brute with slavering powerful jaws, its nose close to the ground following his scent. He could see the others now. Four couples. There would be more, but he could wait no longer.

Cautiously, he began the descent. They had seen him now, and there was no time to waste. The ground was soft beneath his steps. His feet sank in a couple of inches or so but it did not impede his progress. Past the spiky grass, beyond the willow and then he was on firmer ground again. He looked behind him. All nine of his pursuers were at the bottom of the slope. Their baying intensified, then suddenly changed to howls of panic. They were floundering. Struggling and sinking deeper all the time.

Reynard stopped and watched them for a few seconds. The flight and the pursuit were forgotten. He was enjoying this. Then he heard the muffled pounding of horses' hooves on the thick carpet of pine needles and caught a glimpse of scarlet through the low branches. He delayed no more.

'You're a bloody fool!' shouted the Master of Foxhounds, his usual ruddy complexion even deeper with rage as he cursed the small, ferret-faced whipper-in. 'You know we can't go beyond the "Devil's Dressing Room" and now we've got the whole ruddy pack in here. Let's hope we can

8

get them out before we run into that madman Lawson.'

'That's right. Blame it all on me.' The smaller man had a naturally resentful attitude plus an inborn persecution complex. 'If anything goes wrong, blame it all on the whipper-in. It's bound to be his fault. But Major, there was no stopping 'em. The scent was too strong. Must've been that 'ole devil fox again. The big 'un that's beat us four seasons on the trot. I . . .'

'Christ Almighty!' The Major tugged hard on the reins of the big chestnut hunter causing the animal to rear, almost throwing him.

The smaller man however had dismounted and was preparing to go to the aid of the two remaining dogs that were already up to their shoulders in the mire. Their howls of anguish were a painful recognition of the fate that awaited them.

'Come back, you stupid bastard!' The stentorian command which had so often in the past instilled fear into a platoon of soldiers now stopped the whipper-in in his tracks. 'Nothing can save them now. Go down there and you'll never come back. Nothing ever gets out of the Sucking Pit alive.'

Tom Lawson, the woodman, had witnessed the saga of the hounds unknown to the huntsmen. From that same hillock where Reynard had turned in scorn of his pursuers this swarthy man of gypsy origin had stood and watched. The baying had brought him post-haste from his cottage in the far glade, a rusty shotgun clasped in his massive grimed hands. He was bent on vengeance. He loathed the chase and all those who associated themselves with it. He hated the landed gentry and the bloated plutocrats, even Clive Rowlands the owner of these woodlands upon whom he relied for his wages. Willingly would he have stood by and watched the Sucking Pit claim his employer as yet another victim. Indeed, there was nothing he would have enjoyed more.

Now, in the seclusion of his dilapidated cottage, fragrant with woodsmoke, he could savour the events of the past few hours. Seated before his log fire, it seemed as though the wisps of blue smoke wafting their way up the narrow chimney were providing him with a slow-motion action replay of all that had gone before. He saw again the agonized faces of the two huntsmen as they stood and watched their hounds dragged down into the Sucking Pit, the helplessness of man and beast enacted within a few yards of one another. When the last dog had disappeared from view there was complete silence except for a final gurgle from the pit and a bubble which lasted a few seconds before bursting.

The scene changed again. This time he saw himself. Younger by ten years at least. He carried the bulky sack as though it were weightless, his pose belying its contents. It soared through the air and then seemed to hang suspended for a while until finally it struck that unnatural greenness with a dull thwack. A couple of gurgles and it was gone forever. The bloodstained hessian sack might never have been. Neither, for that matter, the mutilated dismembered corpse inside it. They were gone. Oblivion. Not quite, though. The image of Marie kept returning to him. Sometimes in his dreams. Sometimes in the woodsmoke. He tried to shut her out. It was impossible. That was the outcome of marrying a gypsy girl so much younger than himself. He couldn't stand the pace. She had found what she wanted in the village. Young men who could match her wriggling snake-like body. He could only stand so much. If they wanted her favours now they'd have to seek them in the depths of the Sucking Pit. That was where they all should be anyway.

Again the scene changed. Himself again. Another body. Bolton's this time. Handsome once. Not now. Not when his skull had been split with a felling-axe, slicing it completely in two and showering his brains down on to his chequered shirt and jeans.

Now he saw the police investigations. He'd just adopted an attitude of disinterest knowing full well that the Sucking Pit wouldn't reveal his secret.

'Good riddance!' he had told the sergeant. 'The

11

bitch has gone, and I don't want to see her again, ever. Nor Bolton. Nor any of the rest of the crap she'd been opening her legs for.'

They had accepted his philosophy. They had to. Bolton and Marie had run off together. Somebody goes missing every day. Only a small percentage of them are ever found. It was all too easy to disappear, nowadays. A new place – another name. Mr and Mrs Bolton, Smith, Jones, anything.

The woodman's gypsy blood flowed more freely through his veins now that he had experienced it all again. He was back in the present, here in his cottage with its smell of woodsmoke and stale cooking. An old man's den. Comfortable. Secure in the heart of Hopwas Wood, two hundred acres of conifer plantations on the fringe of the industrial Midlands. A backwater in a sea of progress and mechanization. Its legend was even blacker than his own evil deeds. For instance, there was that area known as the 'Hanging Wood' where Oliver Cromwell was reputed to have hanged one hundred Royalists, leaving their bodies suspended there as a warning to their followers. On windy nights, if you listened carefully, you could hear the creaking of the branches as the hempen ropes swung to and fro, followed by an occasional thud as one of them snapped under the weight, and the corpse plummeted downwards to the thick carpet of leaves beneath.

Few people went there after dark.

Less than a quarter of a mile away, on the southern boundary, stood the 'Devil's Dressing Room' – another place to be avoided by the faint of heart. It was supposedly here that the Devil had paused on his arrival on earth to change into human form. Strange things had been reported by farmworkers on their nocturnal missions to tend their sheep in the adjoining fields. Only the gypsies went there ... and 'Romany' Lawson as he was known to them. The roving bands often used it as a winter encampment, sheltered from the north winds by its tall Scots pines. They had no fear. They were disciples of the Master anyway.

Tom Lawson cut slices of tobacco from the thick roll of black twist and began stuffing them into his charred cherry-wood pipe. Using a glowing piece of wood from the fire he inhaled deeply and only when it was going to his satisfaction did he allow his thoughts to dwell on Jenny. He saw her as clearly as if she were sitting in the chair opposite. Beautiful features, petite figure, long dark hair falling tantalizingly below her shoulders, immaculate in every detail. Even his aged loins stirred slightly at the vision but he dispelled those provocative thoughts at once. He mustn't think of her in that way. Not Jenny Lawson, his late brother's daughter. The Devil rest his black soul. Bob Lawson was in the Sucking Pit too. That was not Romany's doing, though. Suicide. Another missing person that would never turn up.

Jenny was the only person in the world Tom had any regard for, except perhaps Cornelius, the leader of the gypsies. Jenny wasn't like these village wenches. She was well-mannered, well-spoken ... maybe even a virgin at twenty-five. Jenny never failed to come and see him at least once a month, though she had no reason to. He had nothing to leave her. Except the little black book, and she didn't even know about that. She was just fond of him. It was a heart-warming thought. Even to 'Romany' Lawson.

Time for bed. He stood up and stretched his muscular frame. The room did not seem as steady as it should be. His breathing was more laboured than usual. Maybe it was the thick twist. Perhaps he ought to give it a rest. The pain in his chest. He'd hardly ever known a pain in his life before except the odd twinges of rheumatism. Now it was as though an iron band was encircling his torso, tightening with every second, pressing on his lungs until there was no room to breathe. He was frightened. He had never been frightened before ... except maybe of Cornelius. This was different.

His heart was pounding. Got to get upstairs. The little black book would tell him what to do. Anything anybody ever wanted to know was in there. A step at a time and he should make it. God, the pain! His head swam. Where were the stairs? He couldn't see them. His vision was gone. Blind. His senses reeled at the thought. After everything he had done, gone through, was this the end?

Then blackness, nothing at all . . .

The red Mini bumped its way along the rough road beneath the towering pines. Although almost mid-day it was gloomy amid the trees and the girl at the wheel shuddered involuntarily. Jenny Lawson had never liked Hopwas Wood, hating the two-mile drive from the main road to her uncle's cottage. She imagined wild animals lurking in the dark undergrowth – maybe even such creatures as werewolves and vampires! Her foot pressed down even harder on the accelerator. Suppose the car broke down. Worse still, suppose it broke down on the return journey *after dark*! She wished that she could have persuaded her boyfriend, Chris Latimer, to have come with her. Not much chance of that, though. Chris didn't like Uncle Tom and he did everything to persuade her not to visit him.

'The cottage stinks,' he had told her on numerous occasions. 'And worse still *he* stinks! He might be your uncle, Jenny, but there's *something* about him. I can't tell you what it is but . . . he's the sort

15

of guy I imagine shaking hands with the Devil if he were suddenly to appear.'

'Rubbish!' This was one of the few things over which they quarrelled. 'Uncle Tom's as good as the next man. Just because he lives all on his own in the middle of a wood you think there's something queer about him. Of course the cottage stinks. It's bound to without a woman to look after it. That's what I go there for, to look after him, and if I didn't nobody else would. And *you're* not going to stop me!'

It was always the same. They argued, agreed to differ and Jenny went to visit her uncle.

The sunshine in the glade was a relief. She drove up to the front door and switched off the engine. Silence. It was noticeable and she shivered. Woodpigeons should be cooing, rooks cawing, and there wasn't even a starling perched on the chimney pot at the rear, the one the old hermit never used and these scavengers regarded as a permanent roost and refuge.

Nothing moved.

Jenny stepped out of the car, slamming the door. The noise echoed eerily in the clearing and for a moment she wished that she had remained back at her city flat, warm and in bed with Chris.

'Uncle Tom,' she called. 'It's me, Jenny.'

Only silence.

She tried the door and it creaked open noisily. She opened her mouth to call again but somehow she felt like an intruder in another world and thought better of it. Her instinct was to run, but she didn't. Instead she stepped over the threshold. It was then that she saw him.

Tom Lawson was lying at the foot of the stairs, his face towards her, the complexion a ghastly grey. His features were contorted into an expression of agony and she thought at first he was dead. She thought she was going to faint but somehow she fought it off. His lips were moving in soundless speech.

'Uncle Tom . . .' She looked at him, her mind in a whirl . . . 'I'd, I'd better go and fetch a doctor.'

'Wait,' the croak was just audible. 'Don't . . . don't go.' She knelt beside him to hear him more clearly. 'It's . . . no good. It wouldn't be . . . now. Upstairs . . . by my . . . bed . . . black book . . .'

Tom Lawson was going to die. There was no doubt about that. He knew it. Jenny knew it. Within minutes she was going to be all alone with the most dreadful companion of all . . . Death!

She decided she should humour him and fetch the book. She had never refused him any request yet, so why refuse his very last in this world? Hesitatingly, trembling, she stepped over him and mounted the stairs. As she did so she remembered that he had always been reluctant to let her go upstairs, and she wondered why.

The smell was worse up here. It cloyed her

17

nostrils and she wanted to retch. It reminded her of unwashed bed-clothes, urine and . . . something else. Something evil.

In the gloom, for the single latticed window afforded very little daylight, she saw the book by the side of the grimed and crumpled sheets. It was little larger than the average pocket diary.

Jenny snatched it up. She wanted to get out of this room as quickly as possible, but she was rushing downstairs to meet a new acquaintance, one who forgets none, whether early or late in life: death. He had arrived. There was no doubt about that. The unmistakable aroma hung in the air.

She did not panic. Indeed she felt much calmer now the inevitable had happened. She just stood looking down at her dead uncle. His features were relaxed and there was a half smile about his lips as though the face muscles had retained this posture even after death

Jenny lit a cigarette and the flame of her lighter dazzled her in the Stygian gloom. Outside the dusk was gathering. She must have mistaken the time of her arrival. After all she certainly had not been here more than a quarter of an hour at the most. There were things to be done: doctors and the police must be informed, the place must be tidied up, cleaned, fumigated. She lit the oil lamp. It seemed cosy now. She had never felt this way about the place before. On second thoughts, she would inform the authorities in the morning. Nobody likes being bothered on Sundays. No point in going back to town tonight. She quite liked the idea of staying. Uncle Tom would be pleased. She was sure he knew. Such a pity to cover up that last smile with a rug.

2

'You've actually spent the night *here*, Miss Lawson!' Clive Rowlands exclaimed, standing on the threshold of the woodland cottage. 'Here. Alone. With . . .'

Jenny Lawson, a cigarette jutting from her full red lips, regarded the slightly overweight owner of Hopwas Wood with a scepticism amounting to arrogance. He would have been an exceedingly handsome man way back in his mid-thirties about ten years ago. However affluence had bloated him and muscle was rapidly turning to fat.

For some moments she did not speak. It was Monday afternoon. The police had gone and the undertakers had removed the body. There would have to be a postmortem which would delay the funeral for about a week. And for the next seven days she intended to stay here in her late uncle's cottage. In fact, she had no intention of leaving at all, despite all that Clive Rowlands might say.

'And why not?' She held his gaze unflinchingly. 'My uncle never harmed me when he was alive so I fail to see how he can do so in death.'

'Well . . . er. . . yes, of course. Quite. I see what you mean. Fine, you stop on here for a bit, Miss

Lawson. As long as you like. I know you've got all your uncle's effects to see to. These things take time . . .'

'Thank you, Mr Rowlands.' Jenny's expression gave nothing away. 'Now if you'll excuse me I've an awful lot to do.'

The door was slammed in the landowner's face before he had a chance to reply. He shook his head in bewilderment as he climbed back into his Land Rover. Girls today. No manners at all. All the same Jenny Lawson was quite an eyeful.

Jenny watched the Land Rover disappear into the surrounding woods, a thoughtful look on her face. So that was Clive Rowlands. Not bad. He could have his uses but right now she had other matters to attend to. There was an awful lot of reading in that little black book. Perhaps it was gibberish, the ramblings of a lonely old man, but perhaps it was more. She seated herself beside the window in the living-room where there was sufficient light for her to read by. Slowly she began to turn the pages.

The writing was mostly crude printing pencilled by Tom Lawson – a mass of jumbled phrases which seemed unintelligible. The name 'Cornelius' was mentioned from time to time almost in reverence. Suddenly one particular passage caught her eye. It was headed: 'FOR MAGIC AND POWER. FERTILITY POTION'. She read on. 'To become strong and powerful. Mix hedgehog and

21

shrew's blood. Boil. Drink at the time of full moon. No clothing to be worn during this rite.'

Strangely, the idea did not revolt her. Instead it appealed to her. No longer was she the kind-hearted typist at Tolsons the stockbrokers. She was a woman in search of power. Her character had changed dramatically although she took this for granted. It was as though she had never *lived* up until now. She felt different. And it was a good feeling.

Then she realized that the time of the full moon was now. The Hunter's Moon. The idea of drinking a strange potion in the nude appealed to her. Why not? She felt imbued with power already. Maybe she would gain greater power. Anyway it was worth a try. Two problems though. She needed a hedgehog and a shrew. Uncle Tom would have trapped them easily. There was an assortment of traps in the outhouse. Yet she had no knowledge of how to use them. She would be in more danger of losing a finger than catching her intended quarry. Jenny sat and thought for a while. Her mind returned to her arrival on the previous day. She remembered the piles of leaves blowing about outside in the gentle autumn breeze. Somewhere she had read that hedgehogs hibernate in piles of dead leaves for winter. Perhaps . . . perhaps . . .

She put the book down and went to the out-house where she found a garden fork amongst the varied assortment of tackle. Then methodically she began raking through the leaves. They scattered and blew in the wind as she worked but her mind was centred only on hedgehogs. Ten minutes later she found one. It curled itself up into an even tighter ball as she scraped away its intended winter home and prodded it with the sharp prongs.

Her eyes blazed with a ferocity unnatural to her. She lifted the fork high, paused for a second, delicately savouring the sensation of power and imminent cruelty and then smashed it with unerring accuracy on the defenceless creature's head. Blood spurted bright red on the golden surface. The animal twitched once, rolled over and unfurled.

'Ah!' Satisfaction and pleasure were hers. She had achieved her aim, and above all she had enjoyed the killing. It was her first taste of power over a lesser being. With no revulsion she picked the hedgehog up by one of its legs and carried it back to the cottage. She hummed a little tune to herself, feeling contentment at the kill.

Placing the little body on the draining-board in the kitchen she was pleased to note that the bleeding had stopped. That was good. She could not afford to waste a drop of that precious fluid. She licked her lips at the thought.

A movement outside caught her attention.

Through the dirty window pane she saw something scurry in the undergrowth.

Stealthily some creature was disturbing the mass of dying bracken on the edge of the tall firs. She lit a cigarette and continued to watch. It moved again. Then she saw it. It was Blackie, Tom Lawson's tabby. It had something in its mouth. A mouse? Too small. The nose was too long anyway. And pointed. It was a *shrew*!

Jenny's heart pounded with excitement. Somebody somewhere was on her side. She opened the door, her eyes glowing.

'Blackie,' she called. 'Blackie. Come here. Come on. There's a good boy!'

Blackie's green eyes regarded her with suspicion. Normally he would have come trotting in expecting a tit-bit. Not now. He already had his tit-bit and he wasn't going to risk losing it. With a miaow of dissent he trotted to an open space beneath the trees, dropped his catch, and contemplated it with relish. He would come in when he had eaten.

'Bastard!' The word fell easily from Jenny's lips as she darted through into the living-room. Propped up in the corner by the fireplace was her uncle's rusty old twelve-bore. There was a box of cartridges on the mantelshelf. She picked up the gun. She had never used one before but it seemed natural to do so. She forced the breech open, pushed two shells in, snapped it shut and went back to the kitchen door. Blackie was still there, his meal untouched as yet.

The stock slid easily into her shoulder and the barrels swung to focus on Blackie. He was still gazing at her, puzzled. Her fingers tightened on the trigger, tested its stiffness, then pressed. The recoil slammed her back against the doorway and she had to wait for the smoke to clear before seeing if she had been on target or not, but the agonized feline screams told her that she had. Partly anyway. Blackie's two back legs were virtually severed. His coat was a mass of blood. Yet he was still alive. The gun came up again. Another crashing report. Blackie was dead now, brains and fur scattered over the pine needles, the skull splattered against the trunk of a giant conifer.

Jennifer calmly walked forwards and retrieved the dead shrew. It was still warm. That was good. The blood would be deliciously fresh.

Later, as the saucepan hissed and sizzled on the open range, the moon was rising into the clear night sky becoming yellow, then silver, as the hours passed.

Jenny lay on the sofa completely naked. Her clothes were folded neatly on the chair nearby. She liked being this way. How much more natural it was not to wear clothes. Her hands strayed down her smooth body until her searching fingers touched the matt of silky hair and the warm moistness of her crotch. Her sensitivity was greater than ever before. She needed a man. A *real* man. Not the boyish Chris Latimer. Someone who would dominate her. Take her as a woman should be taken.

A tangy soul-reaching aroma broke into her thoughts. The brew was ready. She stood up and lifted the saucepan from the glowing embers. The potion was bubbling. Deep red. Blood red. The very look of it excited her and as she inhaled its fumes her nostrils flared. She had a fleeting remembrance of acting in a play back in her schooldays: *Macbeth*. Now it was for real

The brew was cool enough to drink. She ignored the mug which she had placed ready on the table. This was no time for niceties! Instead she grasped the charred old saucepan with both hands, tilted back her head, and drank greedily. For two whole minutes she slurped and gurgled and then with an oath she flung the utensil from her. She grasped the table for support, her knuckles showing white as the fiery liquid coursed through her veins. Moonbeams filtered on to her naked body, blood trickled from her lips on to her small firm breasts and her teeth were bared in savagery towards the whole world. She spat. A mixture of blood and spittle. Men. She wanted men! They were the only food which would satisfy her hunger now. Deliberately she began to dress herself.

* * *

The city streets were deserted apart from a few late-night revellers when Jenny carefully parked the Mini and looked at her watch. Twelve-thirty A.M. Late, but not too late.

The pavements felt hard and unreal after the soft ferny floor of Hopwas Wood. The tall office blocks gave her a feeling of claustrophobia. Seldom did an animal of the wild venture into civilized places to seek its prey. Yet she would not have found a victim in that remote rural place. Not tonight anyway, when she most needed one.

The alleyway by the Odeon cinema was her destination, a dark winding passage filtering off New Street. A lot of prostitutes solicited there. Tonight it was empty. Perhaps she was too late after all. Give it ten minutes. She leaned back against the wall and lit a cigarette, opening her sheepskin topcoat in order to display her neat figure. On inspiration she undid the top two buttons of her nylon blouse displaying her breasts down to the cups of her bra. She remembered something Uncle Tom had said once, many years ago, when her father had taken her there on a visit. 'If you want to catch your prey you've got to use the right kind of bait.' Jenny was using that bait now.

There was a constant stream of late-night traffic. A couple of drunks staggered along New Street and Jenny pressed herself back into the shadows. She did not want a boozed-up fumbler. Two policemen. She moved even further back.

Strangely she did not feel the autumnal nip. It was as though her body were heated by an inner furnace, a volcano just waiting to erupt.

The traffic was petering out now and the street seemed empty. Maybe she should go home, but her desires overruled her commonsense. She stayed.

Another half-hour and then footsteps again. More decisive this time. Not hurrying either. Pausing every so often. Then she saw him. He was well over six feet tall and his burnished skin shone in the artificial light like black ebony. He'd do. She stepped out of the shadows so that he could see her. Their gaze met and held.

'Ah!' His expellation of breath asked and told everything.

'Two quid,' she snapped, her voice hard and even, jerking her head at the same time to signify that she wanted to move further back into the alley. He did not speak but his breath came faster as he followed her. She led him into the shelter of a delivery bay adjoining the rear entrance to one of the stores.

Two crisp notes were pressed into her hand and then strong fingers began desperately tugging at her clothes. The fire within her was fanned into a flame as their two bodies mingled into the blackness of the wall.

Five minutes later they parted. He was totally spent, her appetite merely whetted, and it was quite obvious to her that he was incapable of any more tonight. Her body was pulsating. Alive. Insatiable. She remembered something. A taste which still lingered pleasantly on her palate: blood. Rich red blood. The most vital liquid of all. The essence of life itself.

Hastily she pulled her clothes on again. He stood and watched her, making no attempt to dress. Obviously he was still fascinated by the lithe body which had been his for so short a time.

Jenny's fingers closed over something small and hard in the pocket of her overcoat. Her penknife. A present from Uncle Tom on her eighteenth birthday. Gently she opened out the blade taking care not to cut herself for it was razor sharp.

'Come here,' she breathed, leaning back against the wall, confident that he would not refuse. He moved another step closer. Her white teeth flashed in the semi-darkness.

'Show me again!' She was confident of success now.

He used his hand to support that which had been the source of pleasure to her. Proudly. He wished that he could perform again but he couldn't. Too much beer, that was the trouble. Robbed a man of his virility.

'OK?' He dangled it for her delight.

Her movement was too quick for the eye to

follow.The tiny blade rose and fell in one flowing sweeping movement. Steel met soft flesh, bit deep and then was free again. It had been wiped clean on the faded shirt and returned to its owner's pocket almost before the victim began screaming and the blood began pumping down on to the concrete. Massive hands tried to stay the flow, black turning to red in a gruesome colour transformation.

Contemptuously Jenny turned away and the blackness of the concrete jungle afforded her the protection she sought.

As she sat in the Mini waiting for the traffic lights to change on the corner of Corporation Street she saw the first panda car arriving. On the junction of Bull Street she pulled over to allow the ambulance to pass. Futile. All of them. He would be dead long before she hit the A38.

'Really, Miss Lawson.' Patrick Tolson the managing director of Tolsons Limited raised his eyebrows in surprise as he read the slip of paper which Jenny pushed across the desk to him. 'This is really most unethical. Firstly you are absent for three days without so much as informing us of the reason. Then you march in here dressed in that ... that "garb" and promptly hand me your notice. I might remind you that in the terms of your contract you are required to give one month's notice. Therefore I must insist that you continue in your employment until the end of the month. I won't enforce the three days though. However . . .'

'However nothing.' Jenny's tone was crisp, defiant. Patrick Tolson in his entire thirty years with Tolsons had never been spoken to in this way. 'You pay me for what I do. I'm not doing any more so you don't pay me. That's logic. Sod the contract. Right now I'm too busy to argue.'

So taken aback was Tolson that his wrath did not explode until long after Jenny Lawson was down in the street below.

Her next call was at her lodgings where after loading her few personal belongings into the car she presented her startled landlady with a slip of paper similar to that which she had handed in at Tolsons.

Her whole body throbbed with a new zest for living. As she drove away from the city a placard on a news-stand caught her eye. 'SAVAGE MURDER IN CITY. POLICE HUNT FOR SEX-MANIAC'.

She smiled to herself and lit a cigarette. Life was good indeed. Furthermore, it could only get better!

3

The coroner's court was a mere formality. 'Death due to natural causes.' No problem there for Jenny Lawson. She had never been fond of funerals though. However, she attended this one, but the moment the coffin was lowered into the gaping hole she slipped away unobtrusively. There were only three mourners – herself and Mr and Mrs Rowlands, and she did not wish to become involved with them . . . yet.

During the service she had observed Pat Rowlands. She had a similar figure to her own. Petite. A peroxide blonde. A real good-looker but who spoiled herself by a superior attitude. A typical business tycoon's wife. A first class shop-window at any social function but back home . . . Maybe not too hot in bed either.

Jenny laughed to herself as she drove back to the cottage. They would meet later. No doubt about that. It would be stupid to forestall the issue.

She wished she could find another hedgehog and shrew, for the taste still lingered in her mouth and the fire still coursed through her veins. The little black book had not stated how long the potion would last. Would a second brew-up be necessary? She must consult it again. More thoroughly. Read it from cover to cover.

Dusk came and she lit the oil lamp, ate some cold meat and baked beans and then settled down on the sofa prepared to spend the evening reading.

She considered the pages slowly. Mostly they contained remedies for a variety of diseases. Herbal cures.

Suddenly she closed the book. Her ears had detected a faint sound. It was a long way off. Coming closer. She recognized it now. A motor car. She could almost judge its progress. Revving hard to negotiate the sandy stretch on the Lady Walk. Then changing down to climb the steep slope. Slowing down at the bend. Into the clearing. Silence.

Jenny lit a cigarette. Just who the hell was it? Rowlands? She wasn't ready for him . . . just yet.

She heard the car door slam. Then came a couple of knocks on the door. Definitely not Rowlands. He would pound away in an authoritative manner. There was no way of knowing other than by opening the door. She was not afraid. Just curious. Wait a minute or two though. Never appear too eager. It puts one at a disadvantage.

Repeated knocking. Whoever it was would know she was in by the light in the living-room. She crossed to the door, slid the key and lifted the latch. Then she flung it wide.

'Jenny!'

'Chris. Chris Latimer. What a surprise!'

'Why the surprise, Jen. Weren't you expecting me?' Somehow he wormed his way past her into the room. She closed the door and followed him.

'Whatever brings you here, Chris?' She affected convincing surprise.

'What d'you mean – whatever brings me here?' His pride was already deflated. 'Did you think I wouldn't come then, Jen? I'd have come before but the *Star* sent me down to London all last week. I tried to ring you at Tolsons. They didn't know where you were. I guessed. Why ever didn't you get in touch with me?'

'Why, should I have done?'

'*Why!* My god, Jen! If you . . .' Latimer clasped his hands to his head in despair.

'Let's get this straight,' her eyes blazed and her voice was like a whiplash. 'You don't own me. Nobody does. I've decided to come and live here and I don't see what the hell it's got to do with anybody else. Even you!'

'But Jen, think of all there's been between us. We've spent the last year trying to scrape together enough cash to get married.'

'So what?' She moved close to him and thrust her face defiantly upwards. 'I've got my stake. I was lucky. I'm going to stop here and I don't want any bastard trying to horn in on my plans!'

For a few moments he was speechless.

'You just want my body,' she snarled. 'You've had it too good for too long. I dropped 'em for you too easily. I was green. I didn't know men from boys. I do now. And when I have it I want it with a *man!*'

Anger blazed in his eyes. 'So you think I'm just a boy. I'll bloody well show you then!'

A sudden push sent her sprawling back on to the sofa. Latimer was tearing his clothes from his body as he spoke. He did not notice her eyes, glowing with cunning and lust. Her hands were busy too. Undoing buttons. Removing blouse, skirt and tights.

The reporter wasted no time, anger and despair spurring him on. Their bodies locked. He'd see how she liked it rough. Real rough. The sofa creaked, vibrated. His breath was coming faster.

Then it seemed as though the oil-lamp were becoming dimmer. The room seemed colder. Her body was twisting like a snake squirming under him. Somehow she managed to slide from beneath him and push him down under her. Her face hardened and her strength increased tenfold. Chris Latimer realized that whether he liked it or not he was virtually powerless to resist. This was not the Jenny Lawson who had shared his bed so many times in the past, gentle, loving and responsive. This was a crazed hell-spawned bitch delighting in domination – in humiliation for him.

Twice his body was engulfed by the ultimate enjoyment. His heart pounded wildly, but his strength was sapped. He could not go it again. Yet still she drove him relentlessly. And all the time she cursed him.

'I said I wanted *men*!' She eased herself off him and spat contemptuously on his nakedness. 'You've had it, boy. You just wouldn't make it with me.'

He forced himself to sit up. His head swam and he wanted to vomit. He reached for his clothes and his hands trembled violently as he began pulling them on. Jenny made no attempt to dress. Instead she sat in the old wooden rocking-chair opposite, a leg draped over each arm, rocking herself to and fro, taunting him. His eyes focused for a second on her soft pinkness before he turned his head away. He was sick. Sicker than he'd ever been in his life.

He walked to the door and lifted the latch. There was a moment of silence. He did not trust himself to speak.

'Jen.' He looked at the floor as he spoke. 'There's something wrong. What's happened?'

'Wrong?' She let out a peal of harsh sadistic laughter. 'Wrong? Nothing's wrong. With me, anyway. If there's anything amiss it's with you, boy. Go find yourself a nice *gentle* little girl, one who likes to curl up under the sheets and play lovey-dovey. Or else you can go and pay for a bit of *real* experience and then come and see me again when you've got it. It's up to you. But don't get hanging around here pestering me in the meantime!'

'I won't,' he stated flatly, already recovering some of his composure. 'But I mean to get to the bottom of this business. Personalities don't change overnight. There's something dreadfully wrong and I'm not going to let it rest!'

Then he was gone, out into the blustery autumn night. She listened to the sound of his car as it bumped and slithered its way back to the main road, and then silence came again except for the hooting of an owl in the firs behind the cottage.

Jenny Lawson slipped a dressing-gown over her naked and only partially-satisfied body and threw another log on the fire. She was exultant. Victorious. She had power. She picked up her book and settled down to peruse it once more.

Half an hour later her ears again picked up the sound of an approaching vehicle. It did not falter in the sand of the Lady Walk nor did the driver change down to climb the steep stretch. This was a much more powerful engine, a Land Rover. Clive Rowlands without a doubt. She smiled to herself. She had been expecting him ever since the funeral and, well, the confrontation had to come sometime. Better now than later.

Again she did not move when the knocking came on the door. She just sat and relaxed. Only when the impatient pounding became almost incessant did she call 'Come in.'

It was Clive Rowlands all right. He was dressed as befits a country squire, and his Norfolk jacket was unbuttoned displaying the rounded but not obese waistline. He stood just inside the door, closing it behind him with his heel. Jenny did not move or speak but noted the arrogant expression on his face.

'Ah, Miss Lawson,' he began, uncertain whether or not to take a seat but finally deciding to do so even though the invitation had not been forthcoming. 'I was rather surprised to learn that you were still here.'

'Were you?' She was putting the onus on the landowner, forcing him to take the initiative.

'Well ... er ... yes.' Clive Rowlands dropped his gaze. 'I thought that by now you would have cleared up all your late uncle's affairs, sorted out his belongings, etc.'

'I have.'

'Oh ... I see.' He was temporarily at a loss for words. A pause. 'His things still seem to be around. I mean, nothing much has changed. The place is cleaner but I rather thought most of his stuff would either have been carted away or burned.'

'Oh no,' Jenny's voice was soft and husky. 'You see, Mr Rowlands ... Clive ...' and something stirred within him at the casual use of his first name, 'I don't want to get rid of anything that belonged to Uncle Tom. So I just moved my own things in here alongside them.'

His mouth sagged open and a reddish tinge infiltrated his complexion.

'Do I take it then, that you have no intention of leaving?'

'Now you've got it,' she said, incorporating the sweetness of a schoolgirl with the determination of a mature woman. 'I've no intention of going from here. Ever!'

'You're crazy!' He leapt to his feet. 'I've been very tolerant with you but there is a limit. Don't you realize that I've got to find another woodman to replace your uncle? Be realistic. I can't build another cottage for the new man just so that you can go on living here. Also I've got to find somebody pretty quick. There's gypsies coming and going as they please in Hopwas Wood. Your uncle was far too tolerant with them.'

'I wouldn't want to live here for nothing,' she stated, while, apparently subconsciously, toying with the cord of her dressing-gown until the garment opened just enough to arouse an initial interest.

'What d'you mean?' The question was sharp.

'Oh, you know.' Her breasts and thighs were fully exposed now. She was casually confident. 'I could be sort of useful to have around the place.

You could drop in any time you liked. I'd always be here.'

Clive Rowlands knew that Jenny had noticed the bulge in his trousers. His mind was confused. His thoughts turned to Pat. Socially exciting. Sexually dull. He thought of what he wasn't enjoying and that which he might. His heart pounded and his pulse raced. Fancy having her here in his own woods with ample opportunity to call at any time and no ties.

'It could be arranged.' He met her gaze again. 'On what terms though?'

'Mine.'

Her frankness excited him. He sat down again on the sofa. Suddenly his hand located a patch of dampness on the material and looking down he noted the stain. It was drying fast in the heat of the room but he knew what it was all the same.

'What's this?' he asked with a note of disappointment, perhaps even fear, in his voice.

'A boyfriend.' She did not falter in her reply nor avoid his gaze. 'He left about an hour ago. He won't be coming back.'

'He . . . he . . .' Clive Rowlands felt a sudden pang of jealousy. 'You . . . let him do that?'

'I did, ' she sighed, 'but he's only a boy. I want a man!'

She stood up and stretched herself showing him everything that was necessary to ensure the success of her plan. Once again the bait was right.

She turned and walked slowly towards the stairs. He knew that he was expected to follow her. He did.

The bedroom was neat and tidy and being warm and comfortable between the sheets, Clive Rowlands was almost tempted to stop the night. He could always find an excuse for his absence from home and Pat wouldn't really worry anyway. Yet his reasoning told him to tread cautiously, a step at a time. No point in rushing things.

He was tired after his exertions. It had been a long time since he had enjoyed it like that. Such a gentle girl too. Her initial brazenness seemed to disappear the moment they were in bed. She knew what a man wanted. Knew what she wanted too. Not like Pat.

'I said I needed a man.' She cradled her head on his chest. 'I never thought I'd find one so soon.'

The compliment did not go unnoticed.

'You don't get much enjoyment out of Pat do you?' she murmured.

'She's all right,' he said, not wishing to commit himself.

'All right isn't good enough. A woman's got to be one hundred per cent or she's nothing.'

He decided that he ought to be getting back home. She helped him to dress and then put her dressing-gown on again.

'Well,' and she squeezed his hand, 'do I stay then?'

He sighed. 'You know damn well you do. Keep it cool though. I'll be dropping in to see you so don't for Christ's sake get coming up to the house or 'phoning me or anything like that.'

'You can rely on Jenny.' Her eyes were glowing. A sort of greenish hue. 'Oh and one other thing. I'll be needing a bit of cash from time to time. You know, housekeeping and general expenses. Not a lot. But I do have to live.'

He was silent for a moment. Blackmail? Not this one. She wasn't the kind. Every man was expected to contribute something to the welfare of his mistress though. She couldn't be expected to exist on fresh air. He pulled out his wallet and extracted some crisp five pound notes.

'Here's twenty quid,' he said.

'Thanks.' She lifted the latch for him. 'That'll keep me going for a day or two!'

After Clive Rowlands had gone Jenny did not feel like returning to bed. All thought of sleep had now left her and her body was invigorated by the pleasures of the evening.

She slumped back on the sofa and picked up the small black book again. She had almost forgotten its existence over the last few hours. Idly she thumbed through a few more pages, mostly of herbal cures again, but two pages appeared to be stuck together. With obsessive care she separated them. Again there was her uncle's crude printing. Much of the pencil had rubbed off so she held it closer to the lamp in an effort to read it. Most was illegible but she managed to decipher the words: 'SUCKING PIT. GYPSY – GROUND. CORNELIUS – .'

Gypsy 'what' ground? It certainly couldn't be a camping ground. Cornelius again. That must be the name of one of the gypsies. It intrigued her but in the end she had to give it up. Clive Rowlands had mentioned the gypsies. Uncle Tom had let them camp in the 'Devil's Dressing Room', and they were always on the move in and out of Hopwas Wood. Perhaps they would be able to throw some light on the mystery. But not tonight for a drowsiness came over her. She did not feel inclined to go back upstairs and soon she was asleep on the sofa in a deep sleep of contentment. It had been quite a night.

Outside the hooting of the owl faded away. Soon the first woodpigeon began cooing.

4

It was after midday when Jenny awoke. Once more the sun shone in a last reminder of the summer which was past. Her head ached abominably. Maybe she ought to have studied those herbal remedies more carefully.

She went outside for a breath of fresh air. Everywhere was peaceful. Perhaps it was all a dream, the orgies and the killing, but she knew it was not. Her veins still throbbed with the ancient fire of life which she had absorbed. She was as much a slave to herself as Clive Rowlands was to her.

She decided to go into the city again. After all she had some money to spend and there would be plenty more where that came from! She fetched her handbag and opened the door of the Mini. It would be a break to get away for a few hours.

The starter was unresponsive to Jenny's push. A slow whine the first couple of times then dead. The battery was flat. She cursed and went back into the house. That was that! For today anyway. Clive Rowlands would have to bring her a new battery. He might be back tonight. She hoped he wouldn't take to calling *every* night. Once a week would be sufficient so long as he paid up. He wasn't too bad though. She wished that she could have seen him as he was ten or fifteen years ago before the growth of that middle-aged spread.

Pat Rowlands gazed quizzically at her husband across the breakfast table. He looked tired. More than that. Shattered. That meeting of the Timber Merchants' Association must have really taken it out of him last night. It didn't usually. As a rule he was home by twelve, but perhaps they had had a lot on the agenda.

'Late last night, weren't you?' she asked as she crunched on a mouthful of toast.

'A lot on,' he replied, appearing to be more interested in the *Financial Times*. 'Not like it used to be. They've called another meeting for tonight. The export side's growing fast.'

'Well you won't be there tonight,' she countered. 'Or have you forgotten? We're going to The Peel Arms for dinner. It's our Wedding Anniversary – if that means anything to you. If I mean anything to you any more! I just seem to be a piece of furniture these days.' She was close to breaking down. Inwardly Clive Rowlands cursed.

'All right, all right,' he mumbled. 'We're going to The Peel for dinner, although I get the impression that *I'm* the furniture around here. Settled. OK?'

She nodded and began clearing the table.

* * *

45

Jenny Lawson was in a bad humour. Her headache had persisted throughout the day discouraging her from further reading of Tom Lawson's notebook. She had tired of her transistor radio. Above all she had slept her fill and there was little else to do. Life in the country wasn't so great after all.

Her mind returned to that hulking brute whose spent flesh she had severed two nights ago. Her train of thought led to Clive Rowlands. Maybe she would do that to him one of these days. She smiled sadistically at the idea. She could see him now, clutching frantically at the gory remains. Screaming. Maybe it wouldn't come to that though ... so long as he continued to serve her and pay up!

Dusk again. A mist was starting to form. It would probably be thick later on. So what? She couldn't go anywhere until she got a new battery for the car. If Rowlands came tonight she would make him go and fetch one for her from the all-night garage in Lichfield. He wouldn't like that, because he would feel like an errand-boy. Serve the bastard right! He'd have to go though, as he wouldn't get anything until he did.

Her head continued to throb. Maybe it would be advisable not to light the lamp. The darkness was more restful. She felt more at home during the nocturnal hours than she did in the daylight, which was weird because she used to be scared of the dark. Not any more.

Something moved outside. She listened. Silence. Probably a rabbit. They usually feed at night. She heard it again. A footstep? The mist was thickening now. She could see it swirling round the window in the light of the rising moon. Uneasily she crossed to the window so that she could look outside. But it was impossible to see anything.

A sudden click. The latch was being lifted. A scraping. The door opening. Rowlands? His car wasn't outside and he wasn't the type to come calling on foot anyway. Silence again, almost. A heavy breathing. Stentorian. Asthmatic. Whoever it was was just *inside* the door.

Jenny looked for the shotgun. It was on the other side of the room. Whoever had entered by the kitchen door would see her before she was able to reach it, and she would never have time to find a cartridge.

The moon came out from behind the clouds, streaming in through the single latticed pane, bathing the room in an eerie silveriness. It was then that she saw him. He was already inside the living-room although she had not heard him move. His face was towards her. She wanted to scream. Some strange resilience kept her from fainting – just.

She remembered seeing a horror film once, the

first time she and Chris Latimer had been to the movies: *Frankenstein.* This nocturnal visitor could well have been a relation of the monster. He was well over six feet tall and had a swarthy complexion. His hair was black and curly with large mustachios. Large gold earrings dangled from the lobes of his ears. A red and yellow scarf was knotted loosely around his neck, its colourfulness in direct contrast to the rest of his drab clothing.

However it was his expression which caused Jenny to freeze into immobility, having neither the power to scream nor to attempt an escape. His eyes seemed to glow in the moonlight like two colossal rubies overshadowed by his black bushy eyebrows. His nostrils flared wide and his flashing white teeth reminded her of wolf's fangs. He regarded her in silence for a moment in the same way that Blackie had stood over the shrew.

'Where is Tom Lawson?' His voice was deep with a strange sounding foreign accent.

Jenny opened her mouth to reply but the words would not come. It was as though there was a blockage in her vocal cords. Her mind was reeling too, lacking the necessary coordination for speech.

'Speak to me, wench!' he thundered, his puzzled expression changing to one of anger. Deep furrows lined his broad forehead. 'Answer me! Where is Tom Lawson?'

'He's . . . he's . . .,' and she had to concentrate to force the words out. 'He's dead.'

'Dead?' He took a pace towards her and she thought for a moment that he was going to strike her. 'Dead? Did you say he was *dead*, girl?'

'That's right,' she said, trying to pull herself together. 'He had a heart attack . . . a week last Sunday.'

Then the man's whole body trembled. His hands covered his face and the only sound was the quickening of his rasping breath. She watched, waiting.

'Heart attack?' He was talking more to himself than to her. 'Nonsense. It was no heart attack. It was brought on by the potion. Such things are not to be experimented with.'

'The hedgehog and shrew's blood potion you mean?' Jenny was fast recovering her composure. This strange nocturnal visitor seemed to be well acquainted with her late uncle so why should she fear him?

Two mighty hands grasped her tiny shoulders and she thought for a moment that she was about to be hugged to death by an irate grizzly bear. The evil face was thrust close to hers and the fetid breath almost caused her to retch.

'What do you know about the potion?' he snarled. 'What is a stripling like you doing meddling in our secrets?'

'I read it in the black book,' she spat back at him. 'I . . .'

'The book!' he roared. 'Where is the book?'

'There.' She nodded her head towards the table and he immediately released her and snatched it up.

'At last!' he announced with triumph. 'At last I have it. Only once had anyone dared to write our secrets down. A terrible risk. It could have fallen into the wrong hands. That must never happen! I trust I am not too late.'

Before Jenny realized what was happening her nocturnal visitor had flung the small book on to the back of the open fire. For a few seconds it lay there and then the smouldering ashes suddenly burst into hungry flames licking around it, and greedily devoured the book until it was nothing more than charred paper.

'I knew Tom Lawson had recorded our most carefully guarded secrets somewhere,' the man was still apparently talking to himself. 'Only his death has finally revealed it to me.' He turned back to Jenny and once more his hands clasped her shoulders.

'Now. Who are you, wench? You are no Romany. What brings you to our brother's dwelling place?'

'I'm Jenny Lawson.' Her voice was firmer now. 'Tom Lawson was my uncle. I'm living here now.'

'Then you must have true Romany blood in your veins. It is not apparent but it must be so.'

He paused and his voice became a mere whisper. 'Tell me. What have they done with the body?'

'It's in the churchyard of course,' she retorted. 'He was buried there a few days ago.'

'A thousand curses.' His hand clawed the air as though he were in agony. 'A thousand thousand curses upon the fools. His soul is tormented. No gypsy can rest in peace in consecrated ground. Better would it be had they left his corpse to the scavenging crows. Oh, the fools!'

He sat down on the sofa and buried his huge curly head in his hands. Jenny decided that she had nothing to fear from this man, drew the curtains and lit the lamp. Still he did not move. It was as though a terrible struggle were going on inside him. She lit a cigarette and at last he looked up.

'Are you not aware of the place where all true Romanies are buried?' he reprimanded. 'The place where hundreds of us, for centuries, have finally been laid to rest? Do you not know the Sucking Pit?'

'The Sucking Pit!' Jenny was unable to contain her surprise. 'Did you say the Sucking Pit?'

'Aye,' he breathed. 'The gypsies' burial ground!'

Jenny remembered the entry in the book. The word which had been obliterated? It was all too fantastic. Like something out of weird fiction. Only it was true!

'I never realized,' she breathed. 'So that is the secret of the Sucking Pit!'

A sudden thought occurred to her.

'You said my uncle died from the hedgehog-shrew's blood potion. Why? Please tell me, because . . . because I drunk it myself.'

'Thunder and lightning!' He was on his feet, gripping her hard. 'Foolish wench! Oh, you foolish, foolish wench. Better it would be for you to be dead!'

She felt sick and sat down in the rocking-chair looking at the floor.

'Why?' she sobbed. 'Please tell me why it is harmful.'

He was silent for what seemed like an eternity. Then when he spoke again his voice was calmer, more rational.

'It is a drink known only to witches and gypsy rulers,' he said. 'It is the most powerful brew in this world of darkness. The stupid become wise. The frail become mighty. The human body is taxed to its utmost. Everything is strained to its limit. Your uncle learned this secret from me. He became as mighty as I. Yet he sought to become even mightier. He drunk a second dose, I presume. He had talked of doing so frequently although I warned him of the consequences. Obviously my warnings went unheeded. Human frailty was burst asunder by a power it could not withstand. You are already as powerful as you can expect to be . . . and live! It could have killed you. It did not. Another dose most certainly would!'

Jenny thanked Providence that she had not found more hedgehogs or shrews on her second hunt, although perhaps it would have been better if she had. She would be dead now. The consequences of her experiment did not bear thinking about!

He smiled for the first time.

'You are fortunate. You have gained power – and lived. The Master, our most terrible leader, has thrown us together. It is meant that you and I shall lead the Romany peoples to glory. We must overcome *all* opposition. It should not be difficult. However, there is one important task which we must accomplish right away. Brother Tom must be interred in the Sucking Pit!'

'But that's impossible,' she cried. 'He's already in his grave.'

'A small problem. One that is annoying nevertheless. We must take the corpse from there and with due reverence commit it to the Sucking Pit!'

A wave of horror passed through her body like an electric current. Cold fingers were clutching at her heart.

'Oh no!' she gasped. 'We can't exhume Uncle Tom. It's . . . it's too horrible even to think about. Besides, it wouldn't be right . . .'

'It would not be right to leave him in torment,'

he snarled, reminding her of a wild beast. 'You cannot refuse to help me. We are joined together by a bond which cannot be severed. For eternity. Even in the dark world beyond we shall not be separated. There we shall serve. Here we rule. Make no mistake though, if you seek to thwart me I can condemn you to a far worse fate. You will grovel blindly in a world of darkness amongst creatures whose existence is beyond mortal comprehension. Do not cross me!'

'All right,' she murmured and her body trembled violently. 'I'll do as you say. There is just one thing I would like to know, though. Who are you?'

He smiled evilly.

'I am known amongst the Romany folk as Cornelius,' he said. 'I am the long awaited messiah of an oppressed race of people.'

She did not reply. There was nothing to say. Cornelius was going to desecrate Tom Lawson's grave. She was going to help him. Then what?

The mist was even thicker as they stepped outside the back door and crossed to the shed where Cornelius helped himself to a massive shovel and a pick from among the various tackle. Jenny carried a large rubber torch with which to guide her companion. That was the only part which she was required to play in the grisly proceedings.

The churchyard was a mile or so from the

cottage and there was no footpath leading to it. It would have been difficult enough to find by daylight, but their journey had to be made in the dead of night when the thick mist swirled around them obliterating every possible landmark.

However, Cornelius never faltered. He strode boldly ahead with Jenny trotting at his heels. She was surprised at her own physical condition. Normally she would have been out of breath by now but her breathing was regular. Only her companion wheezed.

Away to the right, possibly three or four hundred yards, she heard a creaking and groaning followed by a soft thud.

'What was that?' she whispered to Cornelius.

'That is from the place known as Hanging Wood,' he said. 'Another martyr has yielded to his persecutors!'

She shivered and asked no more. She knew the legend well enough.

A quarter of an hour later they were in the churchyard. Through the mist they could make out the headstones of the graves, sentinels in an encroaching jungle of weeds and briars. Jenny flashed the torch but the beam was merely thrown back at her by the rolling wall of fog. She would not need it yet.

Cornelius stopped suddenly and she bumped into him. Before them was a rectangle of soft earth with no markings except a wreath which she recognized as the one she had purchased the previous week for Tom Lawson.

Cornelius started to dig.

5

Old Ryle had walked almost every stretch of road in the British Isles. He could not remember the time when he hadn't been on the move and for more than fifty years he had never slept with a roof over his head. He didn't like barns and outhouses. They gave him a feeling of claustrophobia. Even in the coldest weather there was always a hedge or ditch somewhere where the wind did not penetrate. Nobody troubled him for he troubled none.

Churchyards were his favourite dossing places. People mostly avoided them after dark so there was always the certainty of a good night's sleep. A folded sack on a tombstone provided a comfortable headrest and more than likely some wealthy corpse would have a fancy monument with an overhead slab to keep the rain from him.

He had been to Hopwas on several occasions. The graveyard was a snug little place sheltered by the deep woods to the north and he had his favourite corner there. He had often thought about taking up permanent residence in it, for surely the Reverend Rogerson, a true man of God, would not turn him out.

Ryle was glad to be back in Hopwas. He would hang about for a week or two. Autumn was his favourite time of year – apart from the mists, because he never slept too well on foggy nights. The slightest sound awoke him. A rabbit foraging after the fresh flowers on the graves . . . or a spade clinking on stones . . .

He stirred restlessly. That piece of stale cheese couldn't have agreed with him. He didn't often have nightmares. Anyway nobody dug graves at night! But he was fully awake now and somebody *was* digging.

He sat up. There was a light about thirty yards away. He rubbed his eyes. He could see two dim shapes: a man and a girl, and there was a pile of excavated earth on the narrow path. The man was standing in a grave wielding something – a pick-axe. Then he heard the sound of splintering wood.

Curiosity had always been a failing of old Ryle's. A man who took an interest in what was going on about him. He'd heard of people who had died of terrible diseases being buried in the dead of night. It called for a careful look-see . . .

There was definitely something strange going on, he decided, as he gained the safety of the large family tomb next to the nocturnal diggers. The big fellow was doing something down in the grave whilst the girl shone the torch for him. Body-snatching maybe. Except that there was no

58

market for fresh corpses these days. It was certainly very strange.

The man was straining to lift something out now. Heaving and grunting. The object was thrust upwards, propelled by powerful biceps. It landed on top of the mound of soil, balanced there for a second or two, and then slowly rolled downwards to rest against the headstone of the family tomb.

Ryle saw it. Recognized it. A shrouded corpse. Then for the first time in his life he panicked. A hoarse croak emitted from his cracked lips as he turned to run. A younger man would easily have stepped over the exhumed body but Ryle caught his foot against it, stumbled and fell on top of it.

His next sensation was of two powerful hands lifting his frail form bodily into the air and then pinioning him against the tomb. The torch shining in his eyes blinded him.

'It's a tramp!' a husky female voice exclaimed in surprise.

'A spy.' The man's voice was foreign-sounding and guttural. 'He must not live to tell what he has seen.'

Ryle tried to scream but the most he could manage was a frightened croak before the sharp point of the pick-axe entered his skull, passed through it, and chipped the granite behind him.

Cornelius wrenched the tool free and struck again. A downwards blow this time, gouging its way from the top of the tramp's skull right down into his throat.

An animal-like ferocity possessed the gypsy. Lying the dead man flat on the granite slab he began to hack and tear with the pick. Blood spurted and trickled. Entrails flew and slithered. It was fully five minutes before he stopped.

Jenny Lawson had watched with delight using her torch to obtain a better view. It brought back memories. She only wished that she could have played a more prominent part in the mutilation. Why not now? A sudden desire transported her from spectator to leading actor. Her fingers located the small penknife in her pocket, its handle responding to her touch like steel to a magnet. The blade was free.

'His silence is assured.' Cornelius turned his evil countenance on her but in the circle of torchlight all she saw was a heap of mangled bloody flesh and cloth. The split skull seemed to smile up at her as she swung her blade downwards, biting deep, twisting and turning, gouging.

But Cornelius caught her by the arm in a savage grip.

'Fool!' he snarled. 'You waste time. Our mission is not yet accomplished. Follow me.'

She was resentful but her companion was not one to be argued with. Reluctantly she wiped the dripping blade on a fragment of cloth and returned it to her pocket.

Cornelius was hoisting the shrouded body across his broad shoulders and staggering back along the narrow path in the direction of Hopwas Wood. The fog seemed to be thickening even more and Jenny switched off the torch, finding it easier simply to follow the plodding form in front of her. The faint moonlight filtering through the swirling opaqueness showed the massive silhouette of Cornelius. He was breathing heavily but it did not slow him down. Twice Jenny stumbled over entwining briars but her companion never halted. He appeared not to notice her difficulty in keeping up with him and she was left to pick herself up and hurry in his wake.

The woodlands were even more forbidding than the silent churchyard. In places she had to judge the gypsy's progress purely by sound, the thick conifers blotting out the moonbeams yet allowing the grey vapour to filter through them. She jumped when an owl suddenly hooted only a yard or so above her head. Somewhere a vixen screeched followed by the answering bark of a dog-fox. It was as though the nocturnal inhabitants of Hopwas Wood were saluting the return of Tom Lawson their guardian in life, now their champion in death.

Suddenly Jenny bumped into Cornelius and staggered back. She cursed to herself but then she realized they were standing at the top of a steep grassy bank. The mist obscured her vision of that

61

which lay below but a faint gurgling told her that they had reached their destination – the Sucking Pit!

Cornelius gently lowered his burden to the ground where it lay in an unnatural position across a tussock of grass. He turned to face the young girl.

'So far, so good,' he whispered, scarcely audible. 'All that remains now is for me to commit him to the Sucking Pit in the manner which is in accordance with the wishes of our Master. Please watch carefully but do not interrupt.'

Jenny felt her heart pounding wildly. Despite her increase in power, at this moment she sensed an insignificance in her presence there. She had no idea what this man intended to do but whatever it was it would not be of *this* world!

Cornelius had advanced a few yards down the slope and now he raised his arms towards the foggy, moonlit sky. Strange incantations poured from his lips in a language which the watching girl could not understand. She thought that perhaps it was ancient Spanish such as might have been used by the ancestors of Cortez. Maybe even centuries earlier than that.

The chant was now rising to a crescendo. Cornelius had his back to her but she could visualize his expression: wild-eyed, evil, he was pleading with someone or some*thing* to aid him in his task. That much was evident. It was becoming colder every second. The atmosphere was almost tangible. The mist closed in and clouds drifted across the face of the moon. It was as though the night air was alive with power and evil.

Jenny shrank back beneath the shelter of a giant Scots pine. She could no longer see Cornelius, only hear his fast, foreign-sounding speech. The blackness was becoming lighter yet the moon was still obscured! Suddenly Jenny knew that they were not alone on the brink of the Sucking Pit.

An ever-increasing bluish haze enabled her to see the whole of this sunken clearing. Cornelius was still in the same place but he had now dropped to his knees. His head was bowed and his whole body was shaking as though with fear.

Fear! Jenny Lawson knew that she had never known fear before. It was as though every vestige of evil from the entire universe was centred in this woodland burial ground. She knew that she was committed to watching whatever was about to happen. Flight was impossible. Nothing mortal could intervene now for the situation was not of this earth.

Something was materializing out of the bog below. Jenny had half expected to see some horned cloven-footed apparition. Not so. It had no form. It was more like a drifting blue transparent cloud. She could see the grassy bank opposite through it. She remembered having read about will-o'-the-wisps on marshy ground, luminous marsh-gas which has led more than one traveller into the quicksands. A Pied Piper who cannot be ignored. She tried to turn her head away but could not. It did not call her but commanded her to watch. Silence. Absolute silence. That was the most frightening part of all. If only it had roared or screeched as spirits invoked in fiction or on the films do it would have been less terrifying, but the very stillness pounded at her brain.

Cornelius slowly rose to his feet, half bowing, subservient. The rustle of his footsteps in the leaves was a welcome relief as he climbed back to where the corpse lay and lifted it with an even greater ease than before. This time he held it way above his head with outstretched arms not even quivering under the tremendous strain.

The mist was thickening again. The dancing blueness was dimming every second. Still Cornelius stood there . . . poised. A gurgling slurping was coming from below as if the pit were a monster demanding to be fed. Only a vague blueness remained which could have been the moonlight once again penetrating the clouds and reflecting the rising fog. The gypsy's knees bent slightly. His biceps flexed. A terrific tautening of muscles throughout his gigantic frame suddenly terminated in a surge of sheer physical human strength. The corpse shot into the air. Upwards, spinning, reached its point of apex and seemed to

64

remain stationary before plummeting downwards. A soft thud. A squelch. Bubbling and sucking. Once more silence. The demon within the Sucking Pit had received its offering and was satisfied.

Blackness and total oblivion for Jenny Lawson. She never even felt the strong arms which lifted her and carried her back through the misty moonlit woods.

It was full daylight when Jenny regained consciousness. The sunlight was streaming in through the latticed window on to her bed. She was fully clothed and it was some moments before the events of the past few hours came flooding back to her. Beside her, lying prone on the floor, was Cornelius. His breathing was heavy but regular as he slept.

Something else was troubling her. She pushed thoughts of what had happened at the Sucking Pit a few hours ago out of her mind and tried to concentrate on the present. Just what was wrong? Disregarding all that had gone before she tried to analyse the present situation. It was a beautiful autumn morning. The sun was shining out of a cloudless blue sky and the birds ... were *not* singing! Nowhere could she hear the warbling of a blackbird or the contented cooing of a woodpigeon. Once again that awful *silence*. Yesterday the woods had been alive. Today they were dead as if in mourning for the final chapter in Tom Lawson's journey to the black beyond.

She decided to get up. As her feet touched the floor Cornelius stirred and his dark eyes flickered open.

'You have slept,' he stated. 'You are rested now.'

'It was silly of me.' She fumbled for her cigarettes, found one and lit it. Then, 'I passed out. I shall have to do better . . . next time.'

He looked at her for several seconds as if searching her innermost thoughts.

'Let us hope there will never be another night like last night,' he said. 'That is the first time that I have ever . . . done that. It was a terrific strain on me . . . and you. It could have killed us both. *He* deemed to spare us . . . because we were doing what was right.'

She drew deeply on her cigarette and regarded him with raised eyebrows. 'I thought you gypsies – we gypsies . . . always buried our dead in the Sucking Pit!'

'So we do. But not like that. The fools. Oh, the fools! Had they not buried Tom Lawson in consecrated ground there would have been no need to . . . to risk our lives. I had to remove the spirit that they had put in him. Or rather I had to call upon the help of one greater and older than I to do so. The Great One is not to be disturbed lightly. Had he thought that our calling was not justified he would have blasted us there and then. If we troubled him again he no doubt would do so. We are fortunate still to be alive. We must show gratitude by carrying on the good work. The glorification and restoration of the Romany peoples to their true place on this earth is our aim. *You* are my greatest ally in achieving this!'

'Me?'

'Yes you. You who have dared to drink the potion and still live. You who have become mighty. You who have the power to ensnare this man Rowlands to do our bidding. Of all places, these woodlands are where the gypsies can gain their power. Not only is the Sucking Pit here but also the Devil's Dressing Room. The Mighty One has his own stronghold there. That is where he first arrived on Earth. From thence shall we Romanies go forward to greatness. We cannot fail. Firstly though *you* must open these woods to the Romanies. They will converge on here from afar. You must go to work on Rowlands. Make him do your bidding.'

'I already have,' Jenny tried to appear as casual as possible. 'I am his mistress!'

The other's face was expressionless. Only his eyes revealed emotion. Jubilation . . . jealousy? He rose to his feet slowly and moved to the window. For some minutes he stood there just looking out. Jenny lay back on the bed. The next move was his.

'Our battle is half-won,' he murmured. 'Soon

the bands of oppressed wanderers can move in here. Security. An island in a sea of persecution.'

'And you,' Jenny's emotions were strung taut as she half-breathed the question. 'What will you be doing in the meantime, Cornelius?'

He took his time in replying. 'There is much for me to do. By day I must remain hidden. Here. It is as well if nobody sees me. By night I can go to my . . . our . . . people.'

'Then you'll have to stop up here,' she replied. 'There's always the chance that somebody might call.'

He nodded his assent. He turned and looked at her. Again only his dark flashing eyes were a key to his thoughts. They saw. They appraised. Even this giant of darkness had an appreciation of beauty.

'There is one other thing. I am not just a man of violence. I fight and kill only because I have to. My needs are the same as those of other men.' He looked at her small beautifully proportioned body as he spoke. 'There is something I need. Only I will not insist if it is against your wishes.'

She regarded him in silence. No longer did he seem an ogre of the night. Physically he was as near perfect as any man she had ever seen. She thought of Rowlands's fleshy body and it repulsed her. Cornelius was not evil. He was a messiah. A people's champion doing only what was required of him.

She began unfastening her clothing.

6

'My God!' Detective Inspector Harman grimaced as he surveyed the mangled human remains scattered over the surrounding tombstones. He wanted to vomit but told himself that he must not. Scotland Yard did not appreciate such weaknesses. Perhaps he should have taken time off for breakfast before he had started out for the Midlands. On second thoughts had he done so he would probably have fetched it all up.

He glanced round at his companions. Sergeant Regan of the CID looked decidedly green. Richardson the local superintendent of police gave the impression that he might have vomited earlier when he had first seen the gory mess but had since forced composure upon himself. The Reverend Rogerson, nearing retirement, was the calmest of them all. He was a man of God.

Richardson was glad to see the two Yard men. It took the responsibility off his own shoulders.

'The experts have been over everything,' he told the detectives. 'They erected these screens as soon as they arrived. I thought that you would prefer to see the scene of the crime for yourself.'

'Who was this man Ryle?' Harman found his

pipe and began stuffing tobacco into it. It was a relief just to do something ordinary, something of everyday habit.

'A tramp.' It was the clergyman who spoke. 'He's been on the roads for years. I've known that he's slept in here on occasions but I've turned a blind eye to it. He's as honest as they come. If he had been a bit cleaner I wouldn't have minded him sleeping in the church.'

'I see,' Harman murmured. He was in his mid-forties now, athletic, and still had a lot of good service to give to the Force. 'And the missing body? A gypsy I believe.'

'Not strictly true.' The Curate decided to join Harman in a pipe of tobacco. 'Of gypsy *origin*. He'd been woodman in Hopwas Wood for many years under a succession of landowners. Did his job. Minded his own business. He wasn't liked though.'

'Why not?'

'It's hard to say. Never did anybody any harm but he was certainly a recluse. He just didn't want anything to do with anyone. Except the gypsies whom he used to let sneak into the woods no matter what his employers said.'

'And so we're left with a mutilated tramp and a missing gypsy's corpse.' Harman turned to his assistant. 'That's a queer blend if ever there was one. A right bloody mess.' He noticed the clergy-

70

man out of the corner of his eye. 'I mean . . . er . . . There's an awful lot of blood about, sir.'

Jenny Lawson began pulling her clothes on. Her hand shook as she lit another cigarette. It wouldn't be true to say that she hadn't been satisfied. Rather she would have liked to have gone on being satisfied. She wished that she would never have to go with any other man again, but she would have to have Clive Rowlands in her bed pretty frequently. Cornelius had made that quite plain to her. She almost vomited at the thought of that which she had once accepted as a hardness. She really would like to dismember him now.

However Cornelius insisted that they played along with the landowner. If anything happened to Rowlands things would be difficult. As long as he was in the palm of their hand everything would be all right. Hopwas Wood would be open to the gypsies. They could live there, have children there . . . die there. It would be an empire contained in two hundred acres.

A satisfied and spent Cornelius had explained everything to Jenny. Rowlands would provide them with money. Freedom. Jenny would have no difficulty in tightening her hold on him. Eventually a Will. A reasonable time and then. . . . There were many ways in which it could be done. Not necessarily murder. He was not in good condition

71

physically. Jenny had heard of out-of-condition horses being ridden to death. She smiled at the thought.

'What is so funny?' Cornelius lying on the bed had noticed her half-smile. 'Am I not good enough?'

'Sure you are.' She sat down beside him and ran her fingers through his curly hair. 'I was just thinking. Screwing Rowlands to death is going to be a novel way of committing murder.'

'You must not rush it. A Will first. Even then it must not be too quick. And ... do you think I shall enjoy you doing it?'

'Of course not,' she tried to reassure him. 'We've a great life ahead of us, Cornelius. We're sticking together. I promise you that.'

He appeared satisfied. He lay back again and closed his eyes. Suddenly he sat up.

'Listen!' he snapped. 'Somebody comes.'

Jenny crossed to the window. A Land Rover was just drawing up outside. Three men jumped out.

'It's Clive Rowlands,' she hissed. 'There's a couple of bods with him who've got "police" written all over them. Quick. Up into the rafters. Stand on the dresser. There's a trap-door immediately above.'

The gypsy pulled himself up into the rafters closing the hatch after him.

'They may not come up here,' Jenny whispered, 'but if they do, not a sound.'

72

She went downstairs.

Jenny Lawson clasped her hand to her mouth in mock horror as she listened to the unearthly story of Hopwas churchyard related by Detective Inspector Harman. She sat down wearily and Rowlands hastened to bring her a glass of water.

'I ... I'll be all right in a minute,' her lips quivered and she buried her head in her hands to hide the faint smile which threatened to betray her act. 'It's ... unbelievable. Whatever would anyone want to disturb Uncle Tom's last resting place for? And ... kill this tramp Ryle? It's too ... horrible for words!'

Harman placed a strong friendly hand on her shoulder.

'I know what a shock it's been for you, Miss Lawson,' he sympathized. 'But we hoped that perhaps you would be able to give us a clue to help us catch these foul fiends. Unfortunately, due to lack of rain lately, the ground's so hard that there were virtually no tracks. No clues. Nothing in fact.'

'But *who* would do such a thing?' she said, wringing her hands together.

'Devil-worshippers!' snapped Harman, tight-lipped. 'They carried out some foul rite last night. My guess is they needed a human sacrifice. The tramp Ryle just happened to be handy. Then they needed a corpse for some other act of black magic.

God knows where they've taken it. Probably trying to call up Old Nick himself with it!'

Shrewd, my friend, very shrewd, thought Jenny. You'll certainly need careful watching. Aloud, 'Is there any way I can help, though?'

'Where were you last night?' Harman asked, trying to appear friendly whilst pursuing his enquiries. 'Did you hear or see anything suspicious?'

'I stopped in all night,' she replied as though pulling herself together with an effort. 'The battery's flat in my car. I couldn't have gone out even if I'd wanted to. I just stayed in and read. Went to bed early. About half past ten. It was very quiet. I didn't hear a thing.'

'I'll see if I can manage to start your car for you whilst you're talking to Mr Harman.' Regan sauntered towards the door, and seconds later she heard the dull powerless whine of the starter.

You're clever too, she told herself. Checking on me and trying to appear helpful at the same time.

'We'll get a battery sent out to you,' the sergeant told her as he came back inside. 'That one's had it!'

'I'll bring her one,' Rowlands said and caught her meaningful gaze for a moment.

'Your uncle was friendly with the gypsies.' This was a statement from Harman, not a question. 'There are signs of them having been in the wood

74

known as the Devil's Dressing Room recently. Seen anything of them?'

'Not a thing.' She looked the Yard man straight in the eye and hoped that he would not go upstairs. Cornelius breathed far too heavily for her liking.

'Well, we're going to get to the bottom of this.' Harman blew out clouds of blue smoke as he talked. 'I can't say I'm too happy about you living out here on your own, Miss Lawson, with a bunch of murdering Devil-Worshippers on the loose. It would be a great weight off my mind if you'd move back to civilization until we've got it all cleared up.'

'Thanks,' she murmured. 'But I can look after myself. I like it out here. I've got this anyway.' She walked over to the corner of the room and picked up Tom Lawson's twelve-bore shotgun, opening and closing the breech with an expertness which belied her appearance. 'Don't get prowling round after dark, will you, Inspector? I might just blast you by mistake.'

Harman smiled.

'I'd watch it,' he said. 'However, I've asked Mr Rowlands here to keep a friendly eye on you. He's coming over with a battery for your car, don't forget. Don't blast him by mistake, will you?'

Jenny Lawson laughed softly.

* * *

Cornelius was safely back in the rafters that evening when Clive Rowlands knocked twice on the back door and staggered in clasping a heavy battery.

'I'll call round and put it in for you in the morning,' he panted. 'Now I really think you ought to keep this back door locked. I'm worried about you with these maniacs at large.'

She squeezed his hand gently and rested her head against his chest.

'I can look after myself,' she murmured. 'I'm shooting on sight from now onwards. It's nice to think somebody thinks something of you all the same.'

His hardness was pressing against her. She dropped her hand and squeezed him through his trousers noticing his expression of delight at the same time.

'Jenny's lover-boy's been thinking about it all day, I bet,' she laughed. Then added in mock seriousness, 'So's Jenny!'

He walked behind her up the stairs, his fleshy hands circling round to encase her small breasts. Half way up she stopped suddenly causing his stiffness to bump into her firm buttocks.

'Oooooh!' she gasped and giggled. 'Come on, Clivey. Hurry up and get those clothes off. Your little girl's simply drooling!'

She noted with satisfaction the haste with which he tore off his garments eager to show her that which would soon be hers beneath the sheets. It was all too easy.

'Phew!' she let out a whistle of admiration as he finally stood naked by the side of the bed. Her hand grasped him lightly. 'It's even bigger than it was the other night!'

He stuck out his chest as well as his stomach. She closed her eyes, turning disgust into delight for her lover's benefit.

'You've made it grow,' he tried to sound romantic. 'I've been walking about like this for two days. Had to wear a pair of baggy plus-fours in order to hide it!'

He did not want to put out the light but she insisted. Much more romantic. You can imagine a lot of other things as well . . . such as the gypsy giant who had lain with her a little over twelve hours ago . . .

Jenny decided to take the initiative more. She had got to put a snare around him which was unbreakable.

The bed creaked alarmingly, threatening the beams of the living-room ceiling. Five minutes and Clive Rowlands' pent-up emotions exploded in hot gushes and his breath came heavily.

'Dammit!' he cursed mildly. 'I didn't want it over just yet. We've only just started!'

She nibbled his ear. 'It's early yet, lover. You can come lots more before it's time to go home. Then you'll have to come again for Pat!'

'Some chance of that. Anyway I don't want it with Pat.'

'She's your wife. It's your duty.'

'Duty be damned. There's no fun in doing it because you have to. You do it because ... because you love somebody.'

Silence.

'Clive?'

'Do you love me. I mean you're ... you're not doing it just because I've got a nice little body that excites you?'

'Of course not. I mean, I'm not doing it because you've got a nice little ... er ... you know what I mean. I love you, Jenny. That's what makes it so awkward.'

'What's awkward about it?' She flicked him with her tongue, determined to keep eager. 'If you love somebody you generally marry them ... or at least go and live with them.'

He sighed despairingly. 'I wish I could. If I was free, Jen, I'd marry you tomorrow. You don't understand. You can't be expected to if you've never been married.'

She appeared to be offended and buried her face deep in the pillow, easily summoning forced tears and choking sobs.

'You men are all the same,' she gulped. 'You can't do without a bit of spare!'

He began kissing her passionately.

'I want you,' his rising desire added strength to his words. 'I want you bad!'

This appeared to quieten her. She was silent for some minutes. Then, 'All right. I'm quite happy to be your mistress on a permanent basis but a girl needs something concrete. I mean a bit of cash is OK. But suppose ... suppose anything happened to you. What would happen to me? Pat would throw me out on my neck. I'd have no home. No cash. Nothing. There again, what if I get pregnant! I'm quite likely to if we keep having it in the raw like this!'

Typical! Clive Rowlands pulled a wry face under cover of the darkness. These birds were all the same. Poke them once or twice and they start screaming about what *might* happen.

'There are things which can be done,' he adopted the tone he kept especially for business clients. 'For instance, I could make a Will. Pat will come into the lot anyway so if I left you the woods and this cottage she wouldn't miss them. I own some quarries on the other side of Atherstone which are worth ten times what this place is worth. She'd have them.'

'Oh, Clive,' she rubbed him fast and gentle in the way he liked, 'that would put my mind at rest. At least I could give myself freely to you then. With my mind at rest I'd be able to do a lot more with you. I'd sort of be your wife. Pat would be

79

your mistress. When will you fix up this Will for me?'

'I'll go into Tamworth tomorrow and see my solicitor,' he promised. 'I'll bring the copy Will and show it to you when I come to fix your battery.'

Seconds later she had rolled him over and was riding him vigorously. He moaned with pleasure. He would sign anything away to have a regular stake in this. Even his soul!

A few feet above them Cornelius allowed a smile of triumph to ease the jealous scowl. Things were really working out.

7

'A fortnight and nothing at all to show for it!'

Detective Inspector Harman looked across the desk in his temporary murder headquarters in Hopwas Police Station at Sergeant Regan. 'Not a bloody clue. The bastards have just vanished into thin air!'

'You'd have thought the corpse would've turned up somewhere,' Regan mused, feeling that his superior was trying to shelve a lot of the blame on to him. 'Usually these cranks take it to use in another rite and then dump it somewhere. It's just as though the earth has swallowed it up. They can't keep it indoors anywhere for any length of time, it had already been in the ground for a week. It'd stink worse than a barrel of Stilton that's gone off.'

'Which makes me think that they've already got rid of it,' Harman snapped. 'Anyway, I've had the AC on the blower. "Enjoying your holiday?" he says; "hate to break it up but there's a child-killer on the loose down in Surrey." That's it, then. Back to London tomorrow. We'll be leaving the case in Richardson's hands. Another unsolved murder for the files in other words.'

'There's a lot of gypsies moving into Hopwas Wood,' Regan stated. 'I've watched four different lots arrive this afternoon. They're camping in that Devil's Dressing Room place. Reminds me of the old Gold Rushes. Sullen bastards. Just ignore you. You know, the old "no speakee English" attitude. What the hell are they suddenly showing up here for? Lawson was their friend but now he's dead they're coming in force. It doesn't add up. I spoke to Rowlands about it. He's another uncooperative bastard. Said he'd much more important things to worry about. Almost like they'd bribed him into letting them camp there. I can't help thinking they've got something to do with this business.'

'Well.' Harman stood up and pushed some papers into a drawer. 'The Chief wants us back and that's that. It's up to Richardson now.'

'These gypsies are becoming a bloody nuisance,' Clive Rowlands complained, sitting on the side of the bed and looking woefully at his limpness. 'I know you've got their blood in your veins, Jen, and I've no particular quarrel with them, but there's a regular army of them in the Devil's Dressing Room. People are talking in the village. They've got the creeps anyway over that business in the graveyard. They're saying that it's the gypsies who were responsible for killing old Ryle and desecrating your Uncle's grave. They're even hinting that I'm in league with them. The Scotland Yard chaps have been asking me about them too. I put them off. Said I was too busy with other things and didn't think they were doing any harm. Harman looked at me like I was screwy! A word to the police and they'd have them shifted pronto. You're putting me in a very awkward position.'

Jenny leaned across the bed and kissed him on the neck.

'Please, Clivey,' she murmured. 'Let them stop. For me. For Jenny who gives it you every night. They're quite harmless and they've nowhere else to go. Uncle Tom would've liked it that way. It's the least we can do for them, isn't it?'

'Well, I'll put up with just so much . . .' Clive Rowlands said quietly. Ten minutes later he had driven his Land Rover away into the night and Jenny Lawson knew that she had won yet another battle. The five pound notes which had been left on the table by the landowner were of secondary interest only.

Breakfast at the Rowlands household was conducted in silence for the third consecutive day. Pat ate mechanically, neither tasting nor seeing her food. Clive was almost unaware of her existence. He could not see her across the table for his *Financial Times* was propped up between the marmalade and the cereal packet.

For some time after the meal was over they just sat there, each busy with his own thoughts, the only sound being the scraping of a match as Clive Rowlands lit a cigarette.

Suddenly Pat stood up, a determined look on her face, and with a sweep of her hand sent the latest stock-exchange prices flying from the table. Her husband looked up in genuine surprise and shock.

'For God's sake!' She was near to hysteria. 'I'm fed up. I can't stand any more of this. Why do we play this game of pretend? Trying to kid ourselves that everything's as it should be. I know bloody well you've got another woman!'

'You're crazy!' He sounded unconvincing for the sudden outburst had taken him by surprise. 'Your nerves are stretched to the limit. It's the atmosphere created by this murder and the business in the churchyard. It'd get anybody down. What you need is a holiday. I think the best thing is for you to go away for a week or two. Go down to your sister's in Cornwall. The break'll do you good. I can manage.'

'Like hell!' and he thought for a moment that she was going to throw a plate at him. 'That'd be fine for you. You'd have her in this house then. It's no good denying it, Clive. I know who it is. It's that little Lawson bitch. There's been nothing but trouble since she's been living in the cottage.

I demand that you get rid of her. Chuck her out. Get the police to evict her if she won't go!'

'Nonsense!' He averted her fiery gaze. 'It's all in your mind. I can't treat a niece of an old employee like that. It just wouldn't be human. And as for having an affair with her . . .' he gave a hollow laugh, 'you've just been letting your imagination run riot!'

'OK.' She was more rational now although none the less determined. 'We'll see. I'm going into town today so you'll either have to eat out or get something for yourself!'

The brass plate on the doorway stated that the second floor of the building comprised the offices of 'Stan Kilby – Enquiry Agent'. The stairs were uncarpeted and gloomy and Pat Rowlands' footsteps echoed as she slowly ascended them and tapped lightly on the door opposite her.

It was the first time that it had rained for a month. The sky had been cloudy all day and now the downpour that had been threatening arrived. The large florid-faced man who had occupied a vantage point in the scrubland adjoining the Lady Walk in Hopwas Wood, cursed fluently.

'Just my luck,' Stan Kilby muttered. 'It hasn't rained for bloody weeks and now the very night I've got to go out it decides to piss down!'

He pulled down the brim of his trilby hat and

turned up the collar of his gaberdine mac. He was
not one to be discouraged. A night-long vigil was
routine to him. More often than not it turned out
to be fruitless. Then, just when you were getting
cheesed off, something turned up and made it all
worthwhile.

According to Mrs Rowlands his night wouldn't
be wasted. The Land Rover would come along at
about eight o'clock. He didn't even have to follow
it. All that would be necessary was for him to
walk on down this rough track until he came to
the cottage. Hang about for a bit. Try and get a
glimpse of them having it away if possible. Then
go back and report to Mrs Rowlands. She didn't
even want divorce proceedings. Just proof that
her husband was having a bit on the side. He
smiled to himself. It would have to bloody well
rain!

At ten minutes past eight he heard the Land
Rover approaching and stepped back into the
cover of a rhododendron bush. The twin headlights of the approaching vehicle lit up the dark
forbidding woodlands as well as showing the driv-
ing force of the rain.

It passed him and then was lost to sight round
the bend. He leaned on the trunk of a tree and
carefully unwrapped a length of chewing gum. No
hurry, no hurry at all. According to his client,
Rowlands would be there for the next five hours.
Better let them get started first! Five hours! He

shook his head and thought of his own younger days. He had always been a come-and-go-home man himself . . .

Nine o'clock! Time to move. He wished that he had brought his wellingtons. His shoes and socks were soaked already. Still, it was all part of the job. It would be better to walk on the rough road and keep out of the grass. He judged the cottage would be about a mile away. Damn the rain! Couldn't it just let up for a few moments?

Suddenly he heard a sound from somewhere ahead of him and dived for the cover of the bushes. Somebody was coming! Heavy squelching footsteps. Purposefully heading for a definite destination. Must be. Nobody with any sense would mooch about for nothing on a night like this.

The other was level with him now. He peered and could just distinguish a dim silhouette. A big fellow. Wearing a cape and hood to keep off the rain. Kilby hesitated. Where was this fellow going? He wasn't heading back towards the main road. Where had he come from? The cottage? Anyway, who was he?

As all these questions pounded at Kilby's brain he reminded himself that it was nothing to do with him. Mrs Rowlands was paying him to obtain proof of an affair between her husband and Miss Lawson. This colossal stranger in the night was none of his business. Yet he hesitated. There was plenty of time. The couple in the cottage would be thrusting away for several hours. There would be ample time to follow this man, find out what he was up to, and then return to have a peep at Clive Rowlands laying his fancy bit! Curiosity was Stan Kilby's one real weakness. That was why he was an Enquiry Agent. He found other people's affairs infinitely more interesting than his own.

The big man was easy to follow. His heavy footsteps and rasping breath would drown any noise made by Kilby. Apart from that he was keeping to recognized paths and rides which were considerably more pleasant than tramping through soaking wet undergrowth.

On and on they went. Kilby glanced at the luminous dial of his wristwatch. If they hadn't reached wherever they were going in the next ten minutes he would have to turn back. After all his main duty was towards Mrs Rowlands.

Suddenly the detective realized that he was alone. They had emerged out of thick woodlands and he could see a dim skyline ahead of him where the landscape terminated in some sort of basin. He paused. There was no sound. No footsteps. Not even the deep asthmatic wheezes to tell him where his quarry had gone.

'Oh well,' he tried to console himself and boost his morale at the same time. 'What the hell's it matter anyway. Nothing to do with me. Better get back.'

He felt uneasy. For two reasons. Firstly he was a stranger to these parts. It had been fine following somebody but how the hell did he find his way back to the Lady Walk in this dark, wet and unfriendly wood? Secondly, just where had the man he was following disappeared to? His flesh tingled at the thought. Memories of recent newspaper reports came flooding back to his troubled mind. This wasn't far away from that churchyard where the old tramp had been found mutilated and a corpse had been stolen from one of the graves. That too was none of his business. The police were paid to look after things like that. He'd better try to find the way back.

He began to retrace his steps, but suddenly he realized that he was not alone. It was too dark to see anything beneath the trees but those rasping wheezes were audible again. Only a matter of yards away.

'Who's there?' he heard himself say, his voice sounding distant and most unlike those pompous tones of Stan Kilby which had echoed across many a court-room.

Silence. He wanted to run but there was no point. He did not know where he was going anyway.

'Who's there?' he repeated, with even less confidence. 'I say . . .' An attempt to make peace in case he had offended. 'I seem to be lost. Could you show me the way back to the main road?'

Still silence. He was beginning to panic. He wasn't used to situations like this. What was the bastard playing at?

He decided to press on. Walk quickly. Confidently. He was bound to come out somewhere eventually. He took a couple of steps. His path was barred. Strong arms seized him. He was whirled round, arms pinioned behind his back. A hand closed over his throat.

'What are you hoping to find here?' the whisper was crude, menacing. The grip was relaxed a little to enable him to reply.

'No ... nothing,' he gasped. 'I ... I wasn't looking for anything. Lost my way.'

'Then why did you follow me for over a mile?'

His mind was confused. The bastard knew he had been following him. Might well have seen him hiding in the trees first. He had deliberately led him out here. Why?

'I ... thought maybe you'd show me the way out.'

'Is that so? When you had only to retrace your steps on the track by which you entered the wood to get back on to the main road. You are a spy. A police spy!'

Kilby wanted to shout. Scream for help. Not that there would be anybody to hear him.

'I'm not police,' he whined. 'My God! I hate the bastards! I swear to you!'

The grip tightened. Kilby kicked backwards

with his heels and felt them make contact with the shins of his attacker, but he might as well have assaulted a wall of solid rock for all the effect it had. His eyes bulged, his tongue protruded and then his gurglings were cut short by a sudden snap which brought instant relief from both pain and fear. Oblivion.

Cornelius lowered the dead man to the ground. He stood and surveyed the body picking out every detail in spite of the darkness.

Fool! Only a fool would think of following Cornelius undetected in a wood at night. Even had he not spotted him crouching in the bushes bordering the Lady Walk the chances of the detective's success were infinitesimal. No, he did not resemble a police spy. If he was he would have been physically fitter and more stealthy in his shadowing. The killing would not have been quite so easy although the result would have been the same in the end. He would talk to Jenny about it later after Clive Rowlands had gone. Right now though the body would have to be disposed of. That was certainly no problem. Indeed that was why he had led him to the Sucking Pit. Why carry him over a mile when he could be persuaded to walk there himself to his own grave?

Cornelius stood on the brink of the pit, the dead detective cradled almost lovingly in his arms. He lifted him high above his head and then hurled him as far out as he could. There followed the inevitable thud, squelch, slurp and a final gurgling before complete silence.

Cornelius turned away and smiled to himself. It was much easier this time. There was no need to call upon one mightier than himself in order that his offering might be received. A morsel such as this was taken as a matter of course.

Police Superintendent Richardson turned to Sergeant Williams with a puzzled frown.

'Another missing person, sergeant,' he murmured. 'A live one this time – Kilby, the private eye. Nothing very startling though. A bachelor. No next of kin. Worked entirely on his own. Hasn't been seen at his office since last Tuesday. The landlord of the block where he has his office gave me a ring. Nothing to get excited about. These blokes often go off on a case for weeks without saying anything to anybody. Nobody likes them. Even their clients despise them. Anyway we'll just bear it in mind. If he hasn't showed up in a few weeks we'll make a few enquiries.' He smiled. 'He's probably run off with one of his clients!'

8

Pat Rowlands was worried. There had been no word from Stan Kilby. Twice she had been to his office and on both occasions it was locked up and there was a permanently deserted air about the place. Maybe it was just her female intuition but she had a strange feeling that she would never see the private eye again and nor would anybody else. It was a disturbing thought. Had he gone off to Hopwas Wood to make enquiries for her or had he left town on an entirely different case? The fact that he did not possess a car meant that the tracking of his movements was that much more difficult. No doubt if anything serious had happened to him the police would find out in due course. She was reluctant to go to them and confess that she had hired him to obtain proof of her husband's adultery. After all, Clive Rowlands was a prominent person in this part of the Midlands. It would not look good for either of them.

Clive Rowlands was absent from home even more as the weeks rolled by. Sometimes he would not even return from his city office in the evening. Instead either the Jaguar or the Land Rover would be parked at the rear of that small woodland cottage by six o'clock. Pat was fortunate if she saw him before midnight. Usually it was after 1 A.M.

The disappearance of Stan Kilby caused no more than a passing interest. The police listed him in the 'missing persons file' and soon he was forgotten. Likewise, the murder of Ryle and the desecrated grave of Tom Lawson became history. The case remained open but more recent crimes demanded the attention of the law. Yet Hopwas village did not forget. The people preferred to remain indoors after dark and speculation was still rife. New lots of gypsies arrived weekly to join those already encamped in the Devil's Dressing Room. Others preferred the neighbouring shelter of the Hanging Wood. And still Clive Rowlands made no attempt to evict them.

A fortnight before Christmas Pat Rowlands decided that something must be done. Kilby had failed her. She knew not why. She had lost her faith in private detectives. There was only one thing to do. She must go herself to the cottage in the woods, confront the lovers, and bring matters to a head. Things could not go on any longer.

A full moon slowly rose over the extensive conifer plantations. Orange at first, then yellow, then silver. By eleven o'clock the countryside was as bright as day. Clive had not returned home. Pat looked out of the window on the countryside surrounding their village house. Tonight was to be the night. Half an hour's walk would bring her to the cottage. A quick reconnaissance would soon tell her whether her husband was there or not. And then . . .

She did not relish the idea of a moonlit walk through the woods. She had heard all the rumours in the village. Devil-worshippers. Human sacrifice. Body-snatchers. Not to mention bands of cut-throat gypsies. It was not a pleasant prospect. All the doubts and fears of the past weeks filled her mind, but she pushed them to one side. If she heeded her fears things could go on like this for months, even years.

Pat had to pass the churchyard en route. It seemed peaceful enough. All the same her step quickened until she felt the soft carpet of pine needles beneath her feet. It was very quiet. The cracking of a twig snapped like a pistol shot in the eerie stillness. She picked her way more carefully. If anybody was abroad tonight there was no point in advertising her own presence.

The paths through the masses of dying bracken were well-trodden for which she was grateful. Occasionally she heard the rustle of a rabbit or a hare and jumped instinctively. She would be glad indeed when this night was over.

Already the hoar frost was forming on the undergrowth, glistening in the moonlight. Yet the beauty was lost on her. It was a relief to step on to the wide Lady Walk. Tyre tracks were evident in the soft sand. Even her unpractised eye could identify them, some obliterating the others. The Land Rover, the Jaguar and that young bitch's Mini! Subconsciously she stamped her foot on the latter. These imprints in the sand told the story as vividly as if she were reading it in a book.

Then she saw the cottage. Dark and silent it stood in the centre of the clearing. No light showed from any of the small latticed windows. Indeed she would have been prepared to have believed that Jenny and Clive had gone out somewhere for the evening had she not seen the white Jaguar parked beneath the belt of firs. So he was here. Probably in bed with the dirty little whore!

She leaned up against the trunk of a large Corsican pine and lit a cigarette. They would not see the glow from here even if they happened to be looking, which wasn't likely. They would be far too busy with other matters.

Her hands trembled. Not from the cold night air but with the sheer fury of a woman scorned. She forced herself to think clearly. Her instincts told her to barge in like an avenging angel. It might work, but ten to one she would be the loser. Should she risk a closer look? Maybe she should let the tyres down. Inconvenience him then present him with the facts when he finally arrived back home.

She stubbed out her cigarette on the bark of the tree. Time to move. Play it as it came. Suddenly her ears caught a faint sound. Somewhere a twig snapped. A hare or a rabbit perhaps. Then another. Something heavier. Her imagination began to run riot. Devils of darkness on the prowl bearing freshly exhumed corpses in search of human flesh and blood ... God! Pull yourself together, girl!

Another stealthy movement from the undergrowth behind her. No doubt about it. *Someone* was there. Furthermore he must have seen her. She would be silhouetted on the outskirts of the clearing. There was only one avenue of escape: the Jaguar. A swift sprint. Clive would probably have left the key in the ignition and the door unlocked. In and away. Clive would have the long walk home. Unless he did not bother to return at all ...

She could hear someone breathing. Whoever it was he had advanced on her since she last heard him. Barely two yards away now. He would probably overtake her and catch her anyway. Better to confront him. Try and stall. Make out she was not alone. If the worst came to the worst Clive would surely answer her screams.

'Who ... is ... it?' The words were a husky croak borne by sheer terror on the frosty night air.

'Don't panic.' The reply was cultured. Steady. 'Keep where you are and don't move. I'll be with you in a second. I won't hurt you.'

The rhododendrons parted slowly. Someone was

emerging, taking care to move as silently as possible. He was still in shadow and she could not see him clearly.

'Sounds carry at night,' he whispered. 'We don't want them to hear us, do we? At least I don't and judging by your own surreptitious approach you don't either!'

He moved clear of the bushes into a patch of moonlight and her fear lessened considerably the moment she saw him. Handsome. Very handsome. Blond hair and in his mid-twenties.

'Name's Latimer. Chris Latimer. Reporter on the *Star*.' He grinned. 'Who're you, anyway?'

'Pat Rowlands.' She felt much more at ease now that she could see he didn't have a pair of horns sprouting from his forehead nor a long forked tail dragging behind him.

'Ah! Clive Rowlands' wife. That explains everything.'

'I'm sorry,' she said, 'but you appear to have the advantage over me, Mr Latimer.'

He offered her a cigarette from a crushed pack and when they had both lit up he motioned her back into the shelter of the rhododendrons.

'They can't see us from here.' He smiled in an attempt to reassure her. 'Now I'd better fill you in on my part of the story. As you are probably aware your husband has been in there for the past four hours succumbing to the charms of Miss Jenny Lawson.'

'The bitch!'

'Agreed. On present form. However she used not to be. Four months ago she was one of the sweetest little girls you could ever wish to meet.'

'Convince me.' Now that her fear was past, her hate for Jenny Lawson was returning.

'OK. I was planning on marrying her! Everything was fine. However the one thing which we disagreed over was her regular visits here to her Uncle Tom. I never liked the bloke. Evil. I can't be more precise, that was just how he struck me. Anyway Jenny came over here one weekend and Lawson died while she was here. Jenny did not come back so I came looking for her. I got the order of the boot. She wasn't the same girl as I'd known a week before.'

He drew hard on his cigarette. Pat Rowlands met his gaze. 'Go on,' she said. 'I'm interested.'

'D'you know anything about "Possession", Mrs Rowlands?'

'Apart from the obvious everyday use of the word the answer is "no",' she replied. 'Anyway, call me Pat.'

'Thanks, Pat."Possession" is something which we cannot hope to understand, only accept. Let me put it to you in its simplest form. If you love someone very much, are part of them in fact, then when they die it is not unknown for their soul to take possession of yours. It's a helluva lot more complicated but that's it in its simplest form. The survivor's character changes. For good or evil. That's what I think has happened to Jenny. She's not Jenny any more. *She's a reincarnation of Tom Lawson!*'

'My God!' Pat Rowlands was obviously very shaken. 'You really figure that is what happened? How much else do you know? About my husband's part in this?'

'Just about everything.' They lit fresh cigarettes. 'It's not just Clive that's involved. It's you and me, these infernal gypsies who keep arriving almost daily, and everybody who lives hereabouts. I've been staying at the Chequers Hotel in the village for the past few days. Making a few enquiries off my own bat. Incognito. I've learned a lot.'

'Such as?'

'Well, with all due respects to your husband, Pat, Jenny doesn't want him just for his love. Or for sex either for that matter. She's playing a very deep game. Take these gypsies for instance. Why's Clive letting them move in on his land like this? I'll tell you. It's because she's pulling all the strings, or to be precise a giant of a gypsy she's hiding in the cottage is. Hopwas Wood is becoming a Romany empire. They're not tinkers either. All of true gypsy blood. I never realized there were so many left in this country.'

'Yes, but what's *she* getting out of it?'

'Probably hard cash for a start. Power. I

wouldn't be surprised if she's got her eye on a whole damn lot more besides.'

'D'you know anything about the theft of Tom Lawson's body from his grave?' Pat asked. 'There was a rumpus here a few weeks back. A tramp was found foully murdered over the open grave.'

'Only speculation,' Latimer continued. 'However I don't think I'm far off the mark. I've been doing pretty well by prowling about in these woods. Well, the day before yesterday an old gypsy died in the encampment in the Devil's Dressing Room. Quite a funeral they held. After dark. Anyway the climax was the throwing of the corpse into that foul bog they call the Sucking Pit. It has some sort of terrible significance for them. It's a sacred burial ground. My theory is that Tom Lawson was given a Christian burial and when these gypsies found out about it they were pretty cut up and went to great lengths to retrieve the body and bury it in what they considered was its rightful resting place. The tramp was just unfortunate. He probably happened to be dossing down there and was murdered to silence him. That Sucking Pit could tell a lot of tales.'

Pat leaned back against the tree for support. 'It's incredible. Something we can never prove. Up until now they've got clean away with it. Even thrown the police off the scent trying to trace a cult of black magicians. Anyway what are we going to do? Bust in there and sort everything out here and now?'

Chris Latimer shook his head slowly.

'I only wish we could. We can't tonight anyhow. For a start there's that murderous Goliath or whatever his name is. He'd probably kill the three of us and we'd all disappear into the Sucking Pit and never be heard of again. If we fetch the police we'll be made to look foolish. We can't prove a thing. At the moment they don't know we're on to them though, which is a definite advantage on our part.'

'It's not much fun knowing your husband's sharing the bed of a ... witch!' Pat was on the verge of despair. 'It's bad enough when you think your man's having it away with another woman. I've gone through hell these past few weeks. God knows my mind must be about ready to snap!'

He slipped a comforting arm about her waist.

'Right now I'll see you home. Don't worry, I'm going to sort something out even if I have to bust in there with a shotgun and take the rap for it afterwards.'

As they sauntered back through the moonlit woods, his arm remained about her waist and he was surprised to feel a familiar stirring in his loins. Something he had not experienced since that last terrible orgy with Jenny. He deemed it wise not to tell Pat about that. There was no point. The feel of her body was not unlike that of Jenny's. Small, firm, desirable. Just blonde instead of brunette.

As they walked on he began to think more about her. It eased his mind after the torment of the past few weeks. He wondered what she was like in bed. Pretty good probably. Maybe a bit out of practice. If Rowlands was having it with Jenny like he'd had it, then he certainly wouldn't have much left for his wife.

They paused at the back door of the big gabled house.

'When will I be hearing from you . . . Chris?' He liked the way she used his first name.

'I'll call round tomorrow evening,' he replied, his hand closing over hers. 'About seven. Unless there's been any drastic changes I've no doubt you'll be on your own. Between now and then I'll be working on something. We'll plan something definite then.'

She was close to tears. 'I just don't know how to thank you. You can count on me to help you in anything you want to do.'

'There's just something I . . . I . . . wondered,' and his voice had suddenly lost its forcefulness. The confidence seemed to have drained away. 'Pat . . . do . . . do you still love Clive?'

She looked up at him and studied his clear-cut

features in the light cast by the full moon above. Their eyes met and held each other's gaze.

'I just ... don't know.' She turned her head away. 'It's something I've wondered for a long time now. I know that he doesn't love me anymore. This isn't the first time he's had other women. The others have just been for a bit on the side, maybe even prostitutes. We haven't ... done anything for months.'

Her face was upturned to his again. Her lips were parted and he could feel her breath. The temptation was too much for him. He drew her to him, his lips meeting hers, his hardness boring against her thighs and she pressed herself closer as his mouth opened to receive the tongue which met his own and probed inside him. His hands felt for her breasts through her coat and she began to moan with desire.

Suddenly they heard the roar of a powerful engine coming down the main road. A screech of tyres as the bend beyond the canal bridge was taken too rapidly then a slowing down as the car approached its destination.

She suddenly thrust herself from him. 'It's Clive!'

'Don't worry.' He flashed her a quick smile. 'I'll go the back way. Make a detour back to the Chequers.'

Their lips met briefly and then he was gone, taking advantage of every scrap of shadow until he was clear of the grounds of Clive Rowlands' country home. It seemed as though a great weight had been lifted from his mind. Maybe some good was going to come of this whole business after all – when the final battle had been fought.

9

Chris Latimer knocked softly on the back door of the Rowlands household. After a few seconds it was opened and Pat stood back to allow him to pass, closing it after him. Her hand found his as she led him through to the living-room.

'Needless to say, Clive hasn't come home. He didn't say a word when he got in last night. A couple of whiskies and straight to bed. Breakfast in silence and straight out this morning. That's the routine now. An atmosphere which I can't break down. I can't stand it much longer.'

They sat down on the sofa and he slipped an arm round her and kissed her. Both were reluctant to break the embrace.

'Of course we could just opt out of it and go away,' he voiced his thoughts as if to himself.

'Oh Chris. Will you take me away from this awful place and all its goings-on?'

He nodded.

'Of course. However we've got to try and sort something out first. You don't want just to leave this fine home and all your belongings for her to move into, do you? There's one thing you must remember. I can't give you anything like this. I'm just a reporter on a basic salary.'

She clung to him tightly.

'I don't care,' she breathed. 'Wealth has brought me nothing but unhappiness and fear. Memories that will take a long time to erase. I don't love Clive. I hate him. I'm in love with *you*, Chris!'

'And I'm in love with you, Pat.' He pushed her back and his hands explored her fully. Her breath was coming faster. It was a long time since she had felt this way.

'What about ... Jenny Lawson?' she asked hesitantly after a while. 'I mean ... you were intending to marry her, weren't you?'

'Once.' His eyes were misty. 'If ... if she were still Jenny Lawson I would probably try to get her back. But she isn't. Jenny Lawson is dead. It is Tom Lawson who lives on. Evil and dangerous.'

'What are you going to do then?' She gripped him tightly. 'I mean ... are you going to leave this nest of evil? Leave them to wallow in their filthy rites and sex orgies?'

He kissed her again. 'I said I'd come to a definite decision tonight. Tomorrow night I shall go to the cottage for a showdown. I shall tell both Clive and Jenny what I know. Also things I cannot prove and then I shall take you well away from here.'

'I want to come with you tomorrow,' she said. 'I want to be there, to make it plain to Clive that there is no other way out.'

Latimer shook his head.

'No,' he said. 'I think it would be best if I went alone. They are evil. It could be dangerous. However, I don't anticipate trouble. I shall just tell them a few home truths. There will be no case of denials from Clive. I shall catch him with his trousers down in the truest sense of the phrase. Jenny doesn't want me anyway. I shall go there at eight o'clock tomorrow night, and should be back here before nine. If you could have everything packed, essentials such as we can get in the car, then we'll go back to my flat temporarily.'

'I want to come with you.' She was adamant. 'It is only right that I'm at your side when you tell Clive we are going away together, isn't it?'

He nodded thoughtfully.

'I suppose so. Maybe I am being over dramatic. I was thinking of that big gypsy fellow. He'll obviously be out of the way though. They're hardly likely to let him sit there and watch them having it away. Clive may not even know of his existence. OK then, we'll go together. No trouble. Just tell them what's what and away. I've got to go into the office tomorrow, but I'll be back here by half seven to pick you up. We'll go in the car. No point in wandering about in those damned woods in the dark.'

She breathed a long sigh of relief.

'I don't know how to thank you,' she murmured. 'Yesterday everything seemed black. No future.

Nothing. Now that's all changed. I've no love for Clive and haven't had for a very long time. I suppose we just stuck together for the sake of outward appearances.'

They were silent for a while.

'Pat . . .' Chris Latimer was the first to break the silence. 'Pat, I'm in love with you. Even if I have only known you for twenty-four hours. These past weeks I've been through hell. I knew I would never get Jenny back, yet I was afraid to tell myself that I didn't want her back. Then after I left you last night I knew what I wanted. I scarcely dared hope. After all, you've been used to all the best things in life and I can't give you any of these. Just a home. Perhaps a family.'

'Oh, Chris,' she drew him down on to her. 'Don't you see that's all I want. All this here means nothing to me. There is no happiness here. I've just lived on dreams, dreams that were shattered leaving me to pick up the pieces. I want to start again, to have a husband who loves me, a small ordinary home and perhaps a family. Will you give me these things, Chris?'

'I'll have a damned good try, anyway.'

She smiled up at him. He knew she was very close to tears. It was only natural for a woman who had been through so much. Silence again for a long time as they just lay there content with each other.

'Chris,' Pat's voice was husky, trembling with emotion.

'Yes, darling.'

'Just ... just in case anything should ... go wrong tomorrow. You know ...' She left the sentence unfinished. 'Will you make love to me now?'

The same thought had occurred to himself but he had not wished to worry her any more, yet apparently doubts were already in her mind and it was up to him to allay them.

'Nothing's going to go wrong.' He smiled encouragingly as both of them began to undress. 'It's just a case of telling the other parties what's what. How they stand.'

'I hope so.'

They were both naked now and there was no embarrassment. No lust. Just a natural desire for each other's bodies. Chris felt that every vestige of tension in his body had been suddenly released. He pushed thoughts of Jenny out of his mind. That last wild sexual union between them. She hadn't wanted him then. Only his body. And he hadn't been good enough. This beautiful blonde girl would not be looking for physical staying-power. She just wanted *him*. Strong or weak.

He kissed her all over and thrilled as she gasped with pleasure. It was also quite evident that she knew how to excite him, too. To make him want the ultimate in this play between two people whose love had emerged amidst an atmosphere of evil.

At last he lowered himself down on to her quivering body and felt the true warmth of her love. Both of them would have remained there for ever had it been possible. Yet their emotions, far beyond their control, refused to linger. They shuddered and gasped as one, and lay for a long time afterwards in sheer contentment.

Once more Chris Latimer had to leave the Rowlands household as he had done the previous night. Keeping to the shadows, he saw the twin beams of the Jaguar's headlights swing into the long drive. Silently he shook his fist at the man behind the wheel. One way or another Fate was closing in on Clive Rowlands. He had had a good run for his money.

For once the city seemed to welcome Chris Latimer. No longer did it seem unfriendly, hemming him in with dull uniformity and oppressiveness. It was almost a relief to walk amidst man-made edifices after the forbidding woodlands which served as a cloak for evil. There was a spring in his step which had not been there for a long time: an appreciation of life. All the same he reminded himself that there was still one more bridge to cross over the river of freedom.

'Hi Chris!' He almost failed to notice Ray Storm, another *Star* reporter jostling in the crowded thoroughfare. 'Enjoying your leave? Thought you'd've left the milling masses for a spell?'

'I've had a few days in the country,' Chris said, not wishing to linger in idle conversation. 'Be back Monday morning. See you then.'

He went back to the flat and did his best to remove evidence of his untidy bachelor-existence in the few hours at his disposal. It would never do for Pat to see it in this state.

Time passed quickly. He would need to start back for Hopwas at 6.30 P.M. at the latest. That would give him ample time to be with Pat at the appointed hour.

At six o'clock he drank a quick cup of coffee and ate some sandwiches. He was not hungry but it would be unwise to face the coming events on an empty stomach. At 6.20 P.M. he drove round to the garage and filled the old Morris 1000 up with petrol. He looked at his watch. 6.28 P.M. Just nice time. He was whistling softly to himself as he joined the A38.

It was only as he approached Shenstone village that he realized something was wrong with the car. It was not pulling. In fact it was losing power. The car behind him was blowing its horn in annoyance as he slowly glided into the kerbside. He swore. Any other time . . .

Chris Latimer had only a very basic knowledge of car mechanics. This in itself was a handicap. Frustration made it doubly so. He would have walked back to the telephone box down the road and called out the AA, but that would have taken another hour at least by the time they had arrived, discovered the fault and rectified it. It was now 7.10 P.M. He pushed up the bonnet and by torchlight conducted an examination of the intricacies of the engine. Loss of power often meant lack of petrol. He knew that his tank was full so somehow the petrol was not getting through. But where?

At 7.25 P.M. He removed the dash pot and saw what was causing the trouble. It was clogged up with oil which had virtually solidified and was badly scored. The needle was sticking. A penknife and his handkerchief were all the tools which he required.

But the task was not accomplished quite as simply as that, for he had to clean it twice before the engine was finally pulling to his satisfaction.

It was 7.45 P.M. when he drove off again.

Two miles further on he spied blue lights flashing in the middle of the road. He eased down and pulled up behind a queue of cars. More cars were stopping behind him. He switched off his engine.

'It's a bad 'un, mate,' a motorist who had been to investigate called out to him. 'Head on. The ambulance is on the way. Nothing's getting through at the moment.'

Latimer was frantic. He considered the idea of reversing and trying an alternative route, but dispelled the notion at once. He was not familiar with this part of the countryside. Especially in the dark. There was only one thing to do: wait.

He sat back and lit a cigarette. He had to take control of his nerves. He felt like screaming.

In the distance he heard the wailing of the approaching ambulance . . .

Pat Rowlands stubbed out her fourth cigarette and glanced at the clock for the hundredth time. Between seven and half past the hands had seemed to stand still. Now they raced. 8.15 P.M.

Where the hell was he? Chris wasn't the type to let you down. Maybe punctuality was not one of his good points but this was ridiculous. She thought about what they had done on this very sofa last night and knew that he would come. But when? She reached for her fifth cigarette.

Then she heard the sound of a car taking the bend down by the canal bridge and coming this way. She leapt to the window, hardly daring to look. It was slowing down. Her hopes rose. But it turned away into another driveway and she felt desolate again.

She sank down into the sofa and wrung her hands in despair. Surely Chris would have telephoned if for any reason he could not make it. He was so determined to force a showdown tonight that he . . .

She stood up, dragging deeply on her cigarette

as realization suddenly dawned on her what had happened. He had been reluctant to take her with him in the first place, but she had finally persuaded him. Now that he had had time to think it over he had decided to go it alone after all! As far as he was concerned there would be no snags. A quick call on the lovers to tell them how things stood and then back down here to pick her up and away.

Hell, she wasn't going to be done out of it like that! The bastards weren't going to get away without the sharp edge of her tongue. She was looking forward to catching them on the job together! She had rehearsed what she would say several times during the course of the day. She felt like an actress who was told at the last minute that her rôle was being cut.

She reached for her coat. Well, they'd get a surprise! Chris Latimer too. On second thoughts she reached for a scrap of paper and scribbled a note. Just in case Chris arrived while she was still away. She placed it on the table in the centre of the room and leaving the door ajar she hurried off into the night. There was no question of fear this time. All the devils in hell would not deter her from the task she had set herself.

It was 8.15 P.M. before the road was finally cleared and traffic allowed to filter through under the direction of an orange-coated policeman.

Latimer swore impatiently to himself as he was forced to travel the next two miles at no more than 30 mph and with no hope of overtaking.

Finally he reached the main Lichfield to Tamworth road and slammed his foot hard on the accelerator. 45 – 50 – 55. The old car was flat out now. He bumped his head on the roof as he shot over the canal bridge and took the sharp bend with squealing tyres. Seconds later he pulled up at his destination. But something was wrong. There was not a single light showing. As he went to ring the bell he noticed that the door was not properly closed and he pushed it open.

'Pat!' he called. 'Pat, are you there? It's me, Chris.'

No reply. He stepped inside and felt for the light switch. Then he saw the note.

'My God!' He crumpled it up and dropped it on to the floor. 'The fool! She doesn't know what she's walking into. Pray God that I'll be in time!'

He drove like a madman, but then the car faltered again. Suddenly it picked up, but just as he turned off the main road into the Lady Walk it petered out altogether. Dead.

He leapt out and slammed the door. It certainly wasn't his night. There was only one thing for it. He would have to cover the remaining distance on foot. Then when he had found Pat they would have to come back and try to get the car going again.

Ten minutes later he saw the cottage in the clearing. He stopped to listen. All was silent. Yet the lights were on in all the rooms. He noted the white Jaguar parked beneath the firs. So Clive Rowlands had not left yet.

He decided on a direct course of action. Straight in through the front door. No time to waste. Pat's life, indeed her very soul, might depend on it. He went forward at a run.

A quick glance through the window showed him that there was nobody in the downstairs room. Everybody must be upstairs in the bedroom.

He thrust the door open and burst in. Then he stopped, clutching at the doorpost for support. The interior of the cottage was a slaughterhouse. Pools of blood were on the floor and bloody handprints smeared the walls. He vomited and then pulled himself together.

'Pat!' he screamed. 'Pat! For God's sake answer me!'

He knew then that there was nobody in the cottage.

10

Darkness had already fallen when Clive Rowlands arrived at the cottage. He was later than usual tonight having come straight from a prolonged board meeting. He was tired and the lines on his face were more pronounced than usual. Jenny greeted him with a smile.

'Hello, lover. Your tea's just about ready.'

He flopped down into the chair.

'Christ! What a day! I'm about all-in.'

'You look flaked, Clivey boy. Not your usual self.'

'I haven't felt too good all today. Had some nasty pains in my chest.'

'Uh-huh!' Jenny affected a worried frown. 'Nasty. That's what happened to Uncle Tom. His was a thrombosis!'

Auto suggestion. The Will was made now. She'd seen the copy. It was time to sow a few seeds.

'Bloody hell!' He sounded worried. 'Don't say that!'

'Oh, it's probably nothing of the kind,' she said, knowing he would think a lot about what she had said. 'Anyway your little Jenny will soon put you right. Take your mind off things.'

He closed his eyes. 'Maybe I'm overdoing it. I was reading an article in one of the Sunday papers which reckoned that sex was a killer. Anybody in their forties needs to go steady. A dangerous age.'

'Oh nonsense.' She put two plates of stew on the table and sat down. 'It's good for you. Revitalizes you. Now get that down you for a start. You'll need all your energy tonight. Your little Jenny's in the mood!'

They ate in silence. For some time afterwards they sat and smoked. Clive Rowlands was depressed. For once he would sooner have gone home.

Jenny pushed her chair back and stood up smiling seductively. 'Shall we adjourn to the upper storey?'

He drew deeply on his cigarette and looked at her.

'Couldn't we give it a miss for once, Jen? I really am knackered.'

She put on a sympathetic expression.

'Tell you what then. We'll go and lie down nice and quiet. Just rest. Maybe talk a little. How's that suit you?'

He nodded and stood up. The stabbing pains in his chest really did feel worse. An hour or two of peace and quiet might do him good. He followed her up the stairs. His shoes and jacket were tossed on to the chair and he flung himself gratefully on to the bed.

Jenny smiled at him and began taking off her clothes.

'Hey!' he snapped. 'I thought we were just going to have a rest.'

'That's right,' her voice was as smooth as honey. 'I just like being in the nude whenever I get the chance. Any objection?'

'No. Aren't you going to put the light off?'

'Let's leave it on for a change shall we? You don't often get the opportunity to *look* at your little girl's body.'

They talked for a bit. He closed his eyes. It was more restful like that. Occasionally she nibbled his ear. Above them she caught a faint wheezing. Cornelius had remarkable control over his breathing when he wanted to. Only once had Clive Rowlands remarked upon hearing something up in the loft and she had dismissed it as mice. The following day the landowner had arrived with a bag of 'Warfarin'. She had impressed upon Cornelius the need for silence and that had been that.

'You're the best I've ever had, Clivey,' she bantered. 'I hope you're not going to pop off suddenly. I don't know what I'll do without you.'

He opened his eyes. 'I'm not ready to go yet. Just a bit tired.'

She was lying on her side facing him, her

breasts within inches of his face. He had never really studied them before. The nipples were large and very firm. He groaned as he felt an awakening further down. It was instinctive, but he wished it would subside.

She took his hand and carefully placed it on her delicate curves. The skin was tender and inviting. She moved it further down, easing her legs apart as she did so. The hair was smooth and silky. That beneath it was warm and moist. He thought his zip would burst. She thought so too and deftly pulled it down.

'No point in keeping it a prisoner, Clivey, when it wants to get out that bad,' she murmured. 'Besides your little girl wants to have a real good look at it.'

She gazed longingly for a while then fell on it with relish. Five minutes later she eased off just in time. Resting back on her haunches she began tugging his trousers off and he was incapable of resisting her.

'Come on, Clivey,' she urged. 'Off with your shirt as well. You know how much I loathe any form of clothing on the job!'

They were naked. He knelt up. He groped. The pains in his chest were forgotten. Instead he throbbed violently. She teased him, leaning back and showing him all that was to be his. He grasped again and she rolled off the bed, dodging him. She darted round the room as he came after her. Finally she let him catch her and hoist her back on to the bed. His breath was wheezing spasms.

'Got you!' he panted triumphantly. 'Now you're going to get it rough. Real rough!'

She laughed to herself as he pounded away at her. It was all too easy. Murder most pleasant.

Finally he erupted, then subsided. He rolled over beside her gasping for every breath. His complexion had a purple tinge. He closed his eyes.

'I could take that again,' she kissed him lightly. 'And again.'

He sat up, grabbed for his clothes and began pulling them on.

'Not tonight,' he rasped. 'All I want to do is sleep. Maybe tomorrow I'll call and see the doctor.'

She watched fascinated as he dressed, making no attempt to cover her own nakedness. She thought of Cornelius up above. She wanted him as well tonight.

Clive Rowlands rose to his feet and made his way downstairs. Jenny followed in his wake not even troubling to pull on a dressing-gown.

'I'll make a drink before you go,' she said. 'There's something I want to talk to you about.'

'Can't it wait until tomorrow night?' He felt desperately tired.

'I'd rather talk now,' she snapped with a trace of irritation in her voice. She placed the blackened kettle back on the remains of the fire and two cups on the table. He sank down into the chair and his weighted eyelids seemed to close automatically. His next recollection was of her shaking him roughly.

'Come on. Wakey-wakey. This black coffee'll do you good.'

He forced himself to sip the strong steaming brew and it seemed to revive him temporarily.

'Well?' he asked, his curiosity aroused. 'What is it you want to ask me?'

'Oh that.' She affected casualness and lit a cigarette before replying. 'It's my birthday next week. I'm twenty-six.'

'I'll reserve a special kiss for you.'

He felt himself coming to life again now. The pains had gone. There was something else though: anger. More than that: fury. He lit a cigarette and made a rapid mental calculation. He estimated that he had handed over almost a thousand pounds already for his pleasures. And signed his woodlands away on his death. He conjured up a vision of Pat. Her body was equal to Jenny's. Maybe it just needed a little coaxing, that was all. A fire that wanted kindling.

'Men *usually* treat their mistresses to something special on their birthdays,' she interrupted his thoughts. 'And at Christmas too. That isn't so far away either. I thought perhaps you'd like to combine the two! It'd save you shopping around twice. And you're such a *busy* man, Clivey.'

He regarded her through half-closed eyelids. 'Go on.'

'Well,' and she drew deeply on her cigarette. 'The old Mini's a bit past it now. I can't get more than sixty out of it, and the clutch is beginning to . . .'

'You greedy little whore!' He spat the words out venomously. 'You've had enough off me to buy yourself another car and plenty left over!'

'Agreed!' Her eyes were glowing strangely. 'But I'm saving for a rainy day. You could well have a coronary you know!'

'You bitch! You'll get no more out of me. You've gone too far this time. You'd better be off this land by the end of the week. Your gypsy friends too. Or I'll get the police in to move the lot of you!'

Her confidence was undaunted. She only smiled.

'Your wife might like details of all that has gone on here, Clivey. I'll bet she doesn't know just how good you are when you get going.'

'She's aware of what's going on,' he countered. 'Confirmation of it wouldn't come as much of a shock to her. I could soon right all that. I've been thinking and her body's as good as yours – only needs the right treatment. She'd respond. Matter of fact I'll give it a try as soon as I get home!'

Jenny threw back her head and laughed. Loud and clear. Taunting.

'You poor, poor fool. You don't really think that you can get rid of me that easily, do you?'

'I'll bloody well show you who's the boss around here!' he snarled and took a pace towards her.

She stood her ground. The smile had gone from her face.

'Hold your ground,' she snapped, 'and listen to this.'

He stopped.

'You remember the boy-friend I had before. The one I sent packing?'

He nodded. 'The one who left his stain on the sofa?'

'That's right. Well, for your information, Mister Clever Conceited Rowlands, I could have him back here tomorrow. Just like that!' She snapped her fingers in the air. 'He'd come running if I sent word to him.'

'Do that, then.' Clive Rowlands was fighting to keep control of himself. He realized now why so many usually respectable, ordinary men committed murders. 'D'you think I'm jealous or something? Go to him. Only keep off my land. You're finished here!'

'Oh yeah!'

Childish play-acting, he thought. Seen too many movies.

'Well, for your information, Clivey boy, he's a reporter on the *Star*. He'd welcome a good story. A real scoop. I can see the headlines now.

125

"Wealthy Landowner Had Gypsy Mistress in his Woods". It'd be a sell-out. Just think it over logically. My requests are very moderate by comparison.'

'You filthy blackmailing little prostitute!' He could control himself no longer. The veins on his forehead swelled and knotted. He lunged forward.

She dodged his first rush and darted round the table. Such items were no obstacle to him now and with one mighty shove he overturned it sending her sprawling. He had been a very strong man in his youth and his strength had not deserted him altogether. There was still a certain amount of muscle beneath the layers of fat.

He pinned her to the floor. His desires were no longer concentrated between the open thighs. That meant nothing to him now. He wanted only her neck between his hands. She screamed.

'Scream away, you bitch!' he shouted. 'There's nobody to hear you out here. You're finished. There's only one place left for you – the Sucking Pit! They'll never find you there!'

Jenny felt blackness engulfing her. Her second scream was merely a throaty gurgle.

Yet her first scream *had* been heard. Up in the darkness of the rafters a huge form stirred. Cornelius wheezed as he lifted the trapdoor and lowered his bulk down into the bedroom below. He moved swiftly in spite of his size, his bare feet making no noise on the floor. The one person in the whole world who meant anything to him was in deadly danger and he would willingly give his life for her.

Clive Rowlands straightened up. That was it. She was finished: dead. He was free. A murderer too but that did not matter. Once she was in the Sucking Pit nobody would be any the wiser. No relatives. If anybody came asking after her – then she had left. He had no idea where. Wasn't interested.

Suddenly he was aware that somebody else was in the room. He whirled round.

Cornelius.

He stood at the foot of the stairs like fury incarnate. His long curly locks were awry and his gold earrings glinted as he shook with anger. Almost inhuman, his eyes glowed and his lips were drawn back over his teeth in a wolfish snarl.

His chest heaved, but his tone was cold and deliberate.

'You have killed her.'

Too shocked to move, or to speak, Rowlands stood as stone.

'You must die for what you have done!'

Clive Rowlands started thinking fast. He always did. It was his greatest asset.

This bastard's got to go too, he thought. Can't leave any witnesses. Get rid of both of them in the Sucking Pit.

He noticed the iron poker in the fireplace and snatched it up.

'Come on then, you gypsy bastard!' he snarled. 'Come and get it!'

Cornelius was no skilled fighter. All his life in matters of violence he had relied upon brute strength and stealth under the cover of darkness. Now he was facing a man who had learned the art of self-defence at public school. Above all, this man was armed and ready to fight every inch of the way for his life.

Cornelius rushed in like an angry bull, head down. Rowlands leaped to one side and brought the poker down with devastating force. His aim was true and it crashed on to the other's skull with a bone-searing crack.

It would have killed an ordinary man. But Cornelius was no ordinary man. Blood trickled from amongst the wad of hair and Rowlands caught him across the face this time. His broad crooked nose split and the scarlet fluid gushed down his cheek and on to his chest.

Cornelius grunted with pain but uttered no threat as he stepped back over the body of his fallen love.

'Not so hot after all, are you?' taunted the landowner, spurred on by the success of his first two blows. 'You should have minded your own business, my friend. Then you would have lived!'

Out of the corner of his eye Cornelius noticed

something lying beside the overturned table. A bread-knife. It had a razor-sharp serrated edge. He stooped for it. The blow which caught him on the shoulder did not deter him. The fight was no longer one-sided!

Rowlands struck again but missed this time. His foot caught against the body of Jenny Lawson and he stumbled.

'Even in death she aids me,' the gypsy murmured, then he struck. Upwards and curving. It caught Rowlands on the hand which wielded the poker. Blood spouted from a severed wrist and he dropped his weapon, recoiling in horror at the sight of his own life fluid spurting high into the air. Clutching at the wound with his other hand he staggered towards the door.

'I have not finished with you yet, my fine friend,' growled Cornelius and thrust again. This time the blade punctured the jugular vein. Rowlands managed to push the knife-arm of his foe away but it was futile. The gypsy merely retired to the far end of the room and calmly watched the final death struggles of the landowner. Clive Rowlands fell back against the wall, his bloody hands clawing at it for support and then slowly he sank to his knees. He tried to speak. Gurgled. Choked. Finally collapsed on the floor and the scarlet flow weakened to a trickle.

Cornelius scarcely looked at him as he sank to his knees beside the lifeless, naked Jenny

Lawson. Automatically his fingers sought her pulse, then her heart, but there was no movement. His head bowed, his body shook and blindly his hand located the fallen bread-knife turning the point towards his own chest. Within inches of his heart, the blade stopped and a strange look spread across the gypsy's blood-stained face.

'Dare I,' he muttered, 'dare I ask the Master to grant me one more favour?'

11

Cornelius did not hurry. There was no need. Tomorrow, next week, next year – it would have made no difference. The length of time which had elapsed since death did not matter. The Master would either grant his request or punish him for asking. Death or worse. It mattered little to a man with nothing to live for. Perhaps it would have been better had he killed himself and joined her in the blackness beyond. If he were certain of their reunion he would have done so, but might he not fail to find her in infinity, just wandering on and on, searching but never finding?

He pulled himself together with an effort. He must have faith. Without it the Master would not hear him. He stopped and lifted the girl's body. She was as beautiful in death as in life and he laid her gently on the sofa folding her arms across her bosom.

Then he paused. It was a terrible thing to do. The very thought was sufficient to drive a mortal out of his mind. The words. He must try and remember them again. There must be no mistake.

He braced himself and then the chanting began. Scarcely audible at first but growing louder all the time. The old words came easily after a while, words of the ancients. Spanish? Even he did not know their full meaning, and had no wish to, for such things are not for mankind. At last he finished. Failure? Success? Hope or despair? He did not know. Nothing moved. Rowlands lay drowned in his own life's blood. Jenny remained still. He had failed. In that case he would take his own life. His lips moved again, but they formed words of his own, not of any ancient rite.

'Master, I beg you to give this girl life. I offer my own, my soul, as forfeit if necessary. I ask this so that we may carry on the work of your people. It is still unfinished.'

Suddenly he felt the atmosphere grow colder. He shivered and then flung himself flat upon the quarried floor. His eyes were shut yet he knew that the light had gone out. Blackness. Icy cold. Then came the blue cloud, that was visible without being seen – it was everywhere. Inside his brain. A voice was speaking to him, yet not through his ears.

'This is the last time. Call me not again. Your plea is answered only so that you may carry on the work which is yet unfinished!'

And abruptly the haze faded, and the darkness came again.

After a time Cornelius struggled to his feet and lit the lamp with trembling fingers. The scene was unchanged. Rowlands, Jenny. Blood everywhere.

Suddenly a movement: a flicker of an eyelid, and Jenny's eyes opened wide and she smiled.

'I saw it all. You slew him well, Cornelius. You risked your . . . everything on my behalf!'

He dropped to his knees and looked at her. She was the same as always. There was no change.

'Pass me my clothes,' she snapped. 'We have much work to do before this night is through.'

He watched her dress. Her body would be his again before long. His alone. This time it would not be shared.

'Firstly we've got to dump that bastard in the Sucking Pit,' she snarled.'Get rid of the body, and clean the place up. There'll be coppers round here like flies tomorrow. They mustn't find anything.'

'Are you all right?' he asked hesitantly.

She felt at her slender throat. The skin was completely unmarked, and there was no pain.

'Yes,' she nodded. 'He did not hurt me.'

'He killed you.'

She shook her head.

'No. I slept deeply. I had a strange dream. I saw you slay him and then . . . somebody . . . else spoke to me. I did not see him though. The voice seemed to come from everywhere and nowhere. It said, "You are rested now. Sleep no more. There is work to be done".'

A sudden thought struck her.

133

'The car,' she snapped. 'We've got to get rid of the Jaguar before morning or we're in a load of trouble. No matter how well we remove traces of him the car will give us away.'

'Perhaps it would be possible to drive it to the Sucking Pit,' Cornelius suggested, never taking his eyes off her for a second. 'Once it is in there it is destroyed forever.'

'No.' She was thinking clearly again now, with a precise, ruthlessness. 'The tyre marks through the undergrowth would be too plain. There would be questions asked which we should have difficulty in answering. That bitch of a wife of his will cause us trouble anyway. We must make it seem as though he was never here at all. There is only one way. I must drive the car away from here. Abandon it somewhere. I must do it now, Cornelius, whilst you get rid of the body.'

'No!' he thundered. 'You must not go out of my sight. I cannot take that risk again. We must be together. The night is young, so there is time for us to take this pig to the Sucking Pit, return here to remove all traces of the killing and then together we will take the car away. I have sworn that we will work together throughout!'

She did not want to start an argument between them so she assented. 'We'd better get moving though.'

* * *

Pat Rowlands felt the fury pounding inside her as she stood on the edge of the clearing and looked across at the cottage. The fears of the night were forgotten. All she knew now was hate; hate for the man who had scorned her love and for the girl who had stolen the last shreds of affection which he might have felt for his legal wife.

Lights were showing upstairs and downstairs. Once she caught a glimpse of Jenny as she walked by the window, naked. The little prostitute! She strained her eyes in an attempt to see what was going on inside, but the latticed windows were small and offered only a restricted view.

She began walking across the clearing. She saw Jenny again, clothed now and standing by the window smoking a cigarette. Casual. Confident. The girl was talking to somebody and laughing. Clive!

Blind anger surged through Pat's body. She wished she had a gun. No, it would have been too easy – too merciful. The bitch was not worthy of a quick death. She would rake her face with her shapely fingernails, so that no man would give this woodland witch a second glance by the time she had finished with her. She ran at the door which whipped back with the force of her body hitting it, and then she was inside.

But she pulled up abruptly, her mind totally unprepared for what she saw. Blood was still trickling down the walls into a congealed mass on the floor, and the body was unrecognizable, but she knew the clothes even in their blood-stained state. She felt horror, but not grief.

Then she saw Jenny – and the other fellow. Horrible. For a few moments her brain accepted everything, telling her she was only a spectator. Maybe it was an hallucination brought on by weeks of brooding. Nobody here *mattered* to her. Clive was dead. So what?

Then something seemed to snap inside her head. She opened her mouth to say something. The words were already on the way. 'I hope you're satisfied now, you bitch.' Instead she started screaming. Hysterically.

Jenny's hand caught her across the face and she staggered back, lost her balance and fell. Her head hit the edge of the rocking-chair and she slumped to the floor. Unconsciousness would have been a relief but she was not to be spared. Instead cold reality took over, and the screaming stopped; she did not even sob, she just sat there. There wasn't anything to say, or if there was she could not think of it.

'Who is this woman?' Cornelius asked.

'This creep's wife.' Jenny nodded towards the crumpled form at the other end of the room.

'She must die then.'

'Of course. Leave it to me for a moment. There are now two to transport to the Sucking Pit. It would mean two journeys. There is no time if we are to dispose of the car as well before morning.'

The eyes of the two women met. Their thoughts were similar which made it all the easier for what Jenny was contemplating. They compared each other, reversing the situations which they had shared with the same man. Both had failed. Now one of them had to be the winner in a final conflict.

'Look at me!' Jenny Lawson was more confident now than ever in her life before. She remembered her sensations following the drinking of the ancient potion. They were increased tenfold now. Nobody in this world would stop her. Even Cornelius was her slave.

'Look at me,' she repeated. 'Think of the man who was once part of you. Recall the union that made you inseparable. Then the breaking of the tie. The transference of that bond to me. We are linked. The flaw in the chain is now broken. We are united in spirit. Only my will is greater than your will. You must do as I say. Implicitly. You must not question me. Our Master commands that we obey him. To do this you must first obey me. *Get on your feet, woman!*'

Pat Rowlands opened her mouth to say something. Somewhere in her haziness flashed a spark of rebellion, but that spark died. She nodded dumbly and struggled into an upright position holding on to the chair for support. Her power of speech seemed to have deserted her.

'You will walk with us into the night. There is nothing to fear. I took your man from you temporarily. Now I am going to give him back to you. You are going to a place where you will be together for eternity.'

Jenny turned to Cornelius. 'Pick him up,' she ordered, nodding towards the body on the floor. He stooped to obey. Blood still oozed from his nose but he did not heed it. Blood was everywhere. It mattered not whence it came.

The dead owner of Hopwas Wood was hoisted on to the giant gypsy's shoulder. Rowlands' sightless eyes hung open almost as though he were seeing them all, the woman who had been faithful to him throughout, the one who had betrayed him, and the man who had killed him. There was a click as his mouth fell back. Maybe he wanted to say something.

Silently they filed out into the night. Jenny led the way unerringly not even having brought her torch with her. Pat Rowlands stumbled behind, blindly and unquestioningly. Finally came Cornelius, his grisly burden slung over his massive shoulders. His breathing was now a harsh snuffling as the blood bubbled in his nose.

It had been a night of blood.

Chris Latimer fought down his panic. He felt better when he had vomited. A check of the whole cottage revealed that there was indeed nobody there. In fact he did not definitely know that Pat had come here tonight. There again, where else would she have gone? Where was she now? Alive or dead? He shuddered at the thought.

He went back upstairs and tried to picture what had happened. There were semen stains on the rumpled bed sheets. Fresh. That much was plain. Clive Rowlands and Jenny. He noticed the open trapdoor above and the footprints in the dust on the dresser beneath. A hidden watcher. The big fellow without a doubt! Somebody had been murdered below. The body had been taken away. Rowlands' car was still outside so the odds were that it was his blood all over the place. Relief set in. Only someone the size of the mysterious Romany would be capable of carrying a dead body for any distance and there was only one place he would have taken it: to the Sucking Pit! Only there would the trace of their crimes be swallowed forever.

He lit a cigarette and pondered on a course of action. He knew these woods well enough to follow Jenny and the man. Yet unless Pat were with them it would be futile. Sure, he could catch them literally red-handed but his first priority was towards Pat. Her safety was paramount. Nothing else mattered.

Then he saw the lime green button, lying beneath the rocking-chair, the thread still attached to it. It had been torn from a garment that he knew – Pat Rowlands' blouse.

He beat his clenched fists on the table in pent up rage and frustration. 'The murdering bastards. They'll pay for this with their own blood. I swear it!'

Visions clouded his mind, dispelling reason: Pat had stormed in here and they had overpowered her, all three of them. Then they had murdered her. And now they were taking her to the Sucking Pit!

'Never!' he vowed. 'Her body shall not rot in there whilst there's life in mine!'

He saw the shotgun and the cartridges above it on the mantelshelf, so he picked it up and loaded it, dropping the remainder of the shells into the pocket of his jacket.

Latimer stepped out into the blackness with murder in his heart.

The old gypsy woman had died just before sunset. It was no shock to her family. A woman of over eighty summers could not have been expected to survive the rigours of the long trek down from the north. Perhaps if they had taken it in easy stages she would have lived ... for a while anyway. Yet it was not a journey over which to linger. They had been called and there must be no delay.

'She is at peace,' her son told the gathering.

They showed no remorse. Death is natural for the human body when its allotted span has been completed. Why mourn something which is inevitable?

'Then we must bury her this night,' an elder said.

'Ought we not to wait for Cornelius?' said the son, unwilling to shoulder any responsibility. The word of Cornelius was law. He was their priest as well as their father.

'There is no need,' the other replied. 'Cornelius would not wish us to wait. Corpses spread disease. Is not instant burial our law?'

'It is so,' the bereaved answered and turned away to prepare the body for its last journey.

They were within a hundred yards of the Sucking Pit when Jenny Lawson pulled up sharply causing Pat Rowlands to bump into her. Her ears had detected the sound of voices ahead.

'What's going on?' she whispered back to Cornelius. 'There's somebody at the Sucking Pit. Police?'

He listened intently. Then he shook his head.

'It is a funeral,' he stated, listening to the chanting. 'It must be Roon. She has been dying for days. Ever since her arrival in Hopwas Wood.'

'What do we do then?' Jenny asked, her temper rising. 'Couldn't the old hag have been buried another time?'

'They are only carrying out the law,' the gypsy replied. 'We must press onwards . . . and see.'

Minutes later they topped the rise and stood on the brink of the Sucking Pit. The light of the full moon showed every detail of the bizarre scene on the opposite bank. About a dozen Romanies were gathered there huddled round a crude stretcher which lay on the ground. A blanket was covering the old woman's corpse. The chanting was slow, almost whispered.

Cornelius lowered Rowlands' body on to some dead bracken. 'They have only just started, so I will go and speak with them. Perhaps they will be agreeable to burying him alongside Roon. It all depends on her son. He has the say and I cannot alter his will. To violate his wishes would only weaken my hold over these people. I can only try and persuade him.'

'What about her?' Jenny nodded towards Pat who stood there transfixed.

'It is difficult,' he said. 'Murder is punishable by death. If they see us kill her we shall not be alive for long. Cover Rowlands' body with your coat. They must not see the wounds or we are finished. I will go and talk with them.'

Jenny watched anxiously as her companion walked round the top of the Sucking Pit and approached the gypsy mourners.

12

'Cornelius!' the elder exclaimed in surprise as their leader suddenly appeared out of the trees.

'Greetings!' Cornelius' expression was impassive. 'Is it Roon?'

'It is.'

'I have another body. I should like to bury it with Roon's.'

'Whose?'

'The man who has given us the freedom of these woods. It is only fitting that he should be laid to rest here.'

'How did he die?'

'His heart was weak.'

'Yet he is not of Romany blood. I must consult the son of Roon.'

Cornelius stood back whilst the gypsies conversed amongst themselves. He tried to remain casual in spite of the torment within him. These people must not suspect. If they did . . .

Finally the elder beckoned him.

'It is the son of Roon's wishes that his mother be buried alone. Had this man been a Romany, it would have been different.'

'We will wait,' Cornelius said and turned away.

'Well?' Jenny Lawson's frustration showed in her voice. 'What did they say?'

'We must wait,' he replied.

Her face was a mask of fury. 'We'll never get rid of that car before daylight! All because of a bunch of ignorant superstitious . . .'

'They are our people,' Cornelius reminded her and she fell silent.

The Romanies were in no hurry to terminate their funeral rites. It was a sacred custom and not to be rushed. For another half hour they continued their low and mournful chanting until the elder and the dead woman's son stepped forward, picked up the stretcher and hurled the body as far out as they could. The funeral was over. Then in single file the party left, heads bowed, retracing their footsteps to the Devil's Dressing Room.

'Come on,' Jenny hissed. 'We've no time to waste.'

Cornelius bent and lifted the bloody corpse out of the bracken once more.

Chris Latimer felt as though his lungs were bursting. Surely it was not this far to the Sucking Pit? Had he missed his way in this eerie wood? Yet the path ahead of him led directly to his destination. There was no turning off.

Voices. He listened again. They were coming this way. Was this the murderers returning having completed their vile deed? He stepped back into a clump of silver birch trees at the same time easing back the hammers of his weapon. He would mow them down ruthlessly. The stomach was the place to aim for. He would leave them there on the path to die slowly.

Nearer now. Amid the Scots pines. Another couple of seconds and they would emerge into that moonlit glade. He raised the gun to his shoulder, his forefinger resting on the front trigger. Now! No, wait! He just checked the final pressure in time.

Gypsies! Maybe he should have fired after all. Perhaps they were the perpetrators of this night's foul deeds.

'Hold it!' Latimer stepped out into the path, the moonlight glinting menacingly on the barrels of the shotgun. 'What's going on?'

The man in the lead stopped and lifted his head.

His voice was no more than a whisper. 'We go in peace. We harm none.'

'I'm not concerned about that.' The reporter's words were charged with concentrated fury. 'I'm just asking what the hell you think you're doing mooching about at this time of night like a bunch of bloody zombies.'

'We have been to bury our dead.'

'What!' The barrels of the gun swung upwards. 'What dead? Speak up, man! Enough of this or I'll blast you where you stand!'

They shrank back in fear. Again it was the

elder who answered him. He was a very frightened man.

'Roon,' he croaked. 'Roon, who has been with us these eighty summers. Her time was nigh. But perhaps it is the other burial you seek?'

'What other burial?' An icy chill was creeping over Latimer.

'Cornelius,' was the reply. 'We made them wait for the dead man was not of Romany blood. You may be too late though for we have walked slowly . . .'

'Stand aside!' Latimer cut him short and the others parted to allow him to pass. He broke into a run. He had never been a praying man, but now he prayed that he might be in time!

Slowly Jenny Lawson descended the steep slope of the Sucking Pit behind Cornelius. The latter, now cradling the dead body as though it was a babe-in-arms, picked his way carefully. One could go safely within five yards of this terrible bog. Beyond that there was no return.

'This will do,' he said.

'Then chuck him in quick!' she snarled. 'We've wasted enough time already.'

With a terrific effort he hoisted Rowlands above his head. The beads of perspiration stood out on his forehead and ran down his face already caked with dried blood. It was as though his strength

146

had been sapped. Only a tremendous will power drove him on.

'Go on,' hissed Jenny. 'What are you waiting for?'

Cornelius heaved. Rowlands hit the mud with a resounding 'splat' and then he was gone. The gypsy turned. He was laughing. Burbling like a child.

'The pit!' he roared, beating his chest like a wild animal. 'The Sucking Pit! That's where we're all going!'

Jenny recoiled, her previous triumph turning to fear.

'Cornelius!' she yelled. 'What the hell's up with you? You're crazy. Stop! I command you to stop!'

But the gypsy's mind had snapped. The strain of this night and his own terrible part in it had been too much for him.

'All together.' His maniacal laughter filled the woodland glade. 'We're all going. To serve the Master!'

A movement amidst the firs at the top of the slope distracted him for a moment. Someone was coming. He hesitated, then he saw the man with the gun, blonde hair awry and a look of savagery equal to his own on the handsome young face.

'Stay where you are, you bastard!' Chris Latimer yelled. 'Another step and I'll blow your guts out! That goes for you too, you murdering little hell-spawned bitch!'

'Cornelius has only one Master!' The giant reached out towards Jenny as she fell backwards up the slope.

The crash of the twelve-bore cut him short. He straightened up. Tottered but did not fall.

'Master,' he called. 'Master . . . Master . . .'

Chris noticed the spreading pool of blood on the big fellow's chest. One and a quarter ounces of number six shot had cut into him at a range of no more than fifteen yards. And still he stood. Towering above the two girls as dangerous as a wounded buffalo.

'Take that, you bastard!' Latimer gave him the second barrel. This time it was a head shot. Brain and splinters of bone flew into the air, but even then he did not fall. A faceless bloody giant – still alive.

Two more cartridges into the breech. A simultaneous double-report. Slowly, very slowly, Cornelius keeled over. The impact of the shot had already carried him backwards to the brink of that terrible burial ground. He slipped into it gently, almost reverently, with scarcely a splash to be heard. Just blood and sucking mud. Then nothing.

Jenny Lawson watched in wide-eyed horror. Pat Rowlands' expression never changed. She had just stood there throughout. Sightless. Mindless. Awaiting her next command.

'Oh Chris!' Jenny forced a note of gratitude. 'I'll never forgive myself . . .'

'Neither will anybody else!' he cut her short. 'You've an awful lot of explaining to do. The police will be glad to get their hands on you. You're going away for an awful long time!'

'You wouldn't . . . hand me over to the police, Chris?' she said with genuine surprise.

'You're bloody right I will,' he snapped. 'Now walk on up here. Slowly. I'm watching every move you make. I . . .'

Her next move was too fast for him. Too unexpected. She grabbed Pat and pulled her in front of her, shielding her own body from the threat of the gun. Jenny's laughter rang out, more taunting, more horrible than that of the late Cornelius.

'Now just hold your horses, lover-boy,' she jibed. 'Your little Jenny isn't quite as soft as that. Shoot and you'll kill us both. Now let's talk terms.'

Latimer slowly lowered his gun. He knew only too well that what she said was true. Above all she was desperate. If she had to die then she would make sure that she took Pat Rowlands with her.

'Talk away,' he said.

'OK,' the reply came lilting back. 'My freedom, nothing else. I could take your fancy bit with me but she would only be a bloody nuisance. She'll never come out of this trance. Ever. Got that?'

The shock of her statement struck him like a

bucket of cold water. His one ray of happiness to be gleaned from this whole black affair would be a mindless robot for the rest of her days.

'In that case,' the threat was empty. 'The best thing I could do would be to shoot you both here and now!'

'But you won't. I know you too well, Chris. You wouldn't even have the nerve to shoot me.'

'Try me and see.'

She bent and whispered something in Pat's ear which he was unable to hear.

'Listen, Chris. Pat obeys my every instruction. I've just ordered her to walk along this bank. She may manage ten yards, maybe two, but sooner or later she's going to fall into the Sucking Pit.'

Next second Pat Rowlands took her first step forward, tottering and uncertain, her gaze unseeing. Then Jenny Lawson leapt and scrambled in the opposite direction gambling on gaining the safety of the trees at the top before he could come to a decision.

Chris Latimer reacted instantly. His gun leapt to his shoulders, the barrels a blur of reflected moonlight as he swung and brought them to bear on the back of the fleeing girl.

'Bitch!' he grated and squeezed the triggers.

Click-click. The sound of the pins falling on spent cases brought a curse from his lips and a triumphant yell from the devil-girl of Hopwas Wood. She had gained a bonus. Even she had not bargained on him forgetting to reload after shooting Cornelius.

He flung the gun down. There was no time to deal with Jenny. Right now Pat needed his help – quickly. Her foot stubbed a tussock of grass and she fell forward on all fours. Then struggled up again totally oblivious of the peril which lay before her. Although she was walking parallel to the Sucking Pit a sideways fall would be sufficient to send her to her death.

'Pat!' he yelled. 'Pat. Stay where you are. Don't move.'

She took another step. His instructions were useless. She did not even hear him. There was only one whom she obeyed.

As quickly as he could he began the descent. The grassy slope was slippery. He dropped on to all fours and began moving 'badger-fashion', thus covering the distance more quickly.

He was within a yard of her when she lost her footing. Headfirst she toppled downwards! He shot forward, fingers grasping. He caught her ankle and held on. The two of them rolled. A yard. Two yards. Then stopped. Six inches away the Sucking Pit gurgled as if in anticipation.

The ascent to safety was accomplished without mishap. He found that Pat was quite happy to be led. He held her hand and she followed in his wake neither assisting nor resisting. Again he spoke to her but her expression never altered.

It was a long walk back to the Rowlands household.

Once clear of the Sucking Pit Jenny Lawson broke into a fast sprint. Her energy was inexhaustible and she needed no pauses to regain her breath.

Her mind was more evil than ever now. Perhaps the death of Cornelius had some bearing on this. Or maybe it was because of the total collapse of all her plans. Dreams of wealth had deserted her, but she still had her *power*. Chris Latimer would pay dearly for his interference.

Two things were uppermost in her mind. Firstly, she needed the cash which was stowed away in the cottage, having spent little of Rowlands' pleasure money. Then flight. She would take the Jaguar. She had always wanted a Jag, but she would have to dump it later of course . . .

The lights were still on in the cottage. She walked in through the open door taking care to step over the pools of congealed blood. At least she wouldn't have to clean it up now!

She fetched the money from the bedroom. A thousand or so in hard cash. It would last for a bit. But there were ways and means of getting more. The Clive Rowlands type was easily caught. The right bait . . .

Downstairs again. The Jaguar was unlocked and the keys were in the ignition, but she had to fetch a cushion from the living-room to enable her to reach the pedals.

It started first time. Purred beautifully. Not like the old Mini. She let it run for a moment. A sudden thought. She went back into the cottage. Some newspapers. Crumple them up. Scatter them on the sofa, add just one match and retire.

She smiled to herself as she let in the clutch. Already smoke was pouring from the open door. She hadn't left much evidence really. Only Latimer. Sod him! She wished she'd never seen him, but she hoped she would again one day.

The car moved off almost silently. After the sandy stretch and the bend it was fairly firm. She pressed the accelerator down a little more. 45 – 50 – 60 – 70 mph. Not bad for these roads.

Then she saw something in the road and slammed on the brake. The cushion slipped. Her foot shot off it back on to the accelerator. No chance. The car standing there in the road stationary was vaguely familiar. A Morris 1000.

A screech of tearing metal followed the impact. Both cars reared. Crumpled. Locked together they rolled sideways down the steep bank. Their progress was halted by the giant oak. It had stood in the Hanging Wood since the days of Oliver Cromwell and it would take more than two plunging cars to destroy it. Another impact. The cars shot back again. Inseparable and unrecognizable as two vehicles. Just mangled metal. Silence.

Dawn. Somewhere a blackbird sung. A woodpigeon cooed.

Sunrise. A dead world was coming to life again. The first time for weeks. None of them knew why. Just wanted to sing again. Life went on.

Dawn was breaking as Chris Latimer led Pat into the living-room. He was exhausted, but she showed no outward signs of tiredness. He would have to sleep. Firstly though he must get help, for she could not be left alone. Of course the police would have to be told. Innumerable statements would have to be made. He did not know when he would have time to sleep.

He walked into the hall and picked up the telephone receiver.

'Chris. Oh Chris!' He dropped it back on to the cradle and dashed back into the adjoining room. Pat was sitting on the sofa, a bewildered, horrified expression on her face.

'Oh Chris!' she repeated. 'That terrible room. Clive. The blood. The gypsies. It *was* all a dream, wasn't it? Oh please tell me it was only a dream, Chris . . .'

13

Detective-Inspector Harman shook his head in disbelief and lit his pipe.

'The mind boggles, Mr Latimer,' he said and leaned back in the easy chair in his temporary headquarters in Hopwas Police Station. 'I never thought I'd be back here so soon. Or for so long. How is Mrs Rowlands?'

'She's fine.' Chris grinned broadly. 'A few days' rest was all she needed. We're getting married shortly.'

'Congratulations.' Harman was no longer the official blustering Scotland Yard detective. Perhaps the successful conclusion to his most sensational case had some bearing on this.

'I must admit,' he went on, 'I was pretty sceptical of your original statements. However our findings since have borne them out . . . and a lot more besides. The strangest factor of all is your future wife's release from the hypnotic trance. According to the pathologist's report the time of Miss Lawson's death coincided with this. It was as though it broke the hold which she had over her.'

Chris Latimer nodded.

The Yard man continued. 'We've had mechanical dredgers working on this place you call the Sucking Pit for the past week. It's almost bottomless. In fact we've gone as deep as we intend going. It's already yielded enough of its secrets. The latest bodies have all been recovered. Besides Rowlands, Lawson and Cornelius we found a man who had been missing for some time: a private investigator by the name of Kilby. How he came to be mixed up with this business the Lord only knows! The deeper we dug the more horrible it became. There were hundreds of skeletons there. I wouldn't be surprised if the Royalists whom Cromwell was reputed to have executed in that Hanging Wood finished up down there. It was a sort of stationary quicksands, contained in one place by the surrounding rock formation. Just how deep it actually goes we'll never know.'

'It's a vile place.' Chris shivered at the very thought of it.

'Was,' corrected Harman with a smile. 'I ordered several hundred tons of rubble to be dumped in it. It kept on taking it. Finally settled though. You can even stand on it now! It was the only thing to do in the interests of public safety.'

'That's the best news I've heard for a long time,' Latimer smiled. 'I haven't been in Hopwas Wood since that last night. Strange to say, though, I've no reluctance to going back there. After all the

Sucking Pit's gone and so has that foul cottage. By the way, are the gypsies still hanging around?'

Harman shook his head.

'There was no sign of them by the time we got there. It was just as though they'd never been: nothing. Not even any mess. Not like these tinkers! Nobody seems to have seen them go either. I guess basically they were harmless enough.'

'I'm just glad it's all over.' Chris pushed back his chair and felt for his cigarettes. 'There's a lot that defies explanation. Things that are better forgotten. Whether Pat will want to continue living here after we're married is up to her.'

'Whatever her choice,' and Harman clasped him by the hand, 'she's only got you to thank for saving her life.'

Latimer shook his head.

'No,' he replied slowly. 'Not me. She's got to thank an old gypsy woman by the name of Roon who chose to die at just the right moment!'

The fox stopped on the edge of the clearing and sniffed the air. Something was wrong. He was puzzled. Yet there was no scent of danger on the warm spring breeze. Nothing stirred.

He moved forward on to open ground. It was very strange. The landscape was flat. There was no basin. No marsh – only soil and rubble.

Reynard had a long memory, for he was getting on in years. He had not been here since the autumn but he still remembered the hounds, their eager baying and then their howls of fear. And the path he had known across the bog, it too had gone. There was no escape route now. To him it was a death-trap! He turned round and set off back through the woods at a fast loping trot.